TYCHO

The most savage, dangerous place on the face of the Moon. Only fools went there to seek their fortune—because no one who went into Tycho ever came out alive.

Chris Jackson thought he was smarter than the rest. He aimed to go to Tycho and come back a wealthy man. But there was one thing Jackson hadn't counted on . . .

Ace Science Fiction Books by Clifford D. Simak

CITY
TIME AND AGAIN
THE TROUBLE WITH TYCHO

THE TROUBLE WITH TYCHO

Clifford D. Simak

ACE SCIENCE FICTION BOOKS
NEW YORK

THE TROUBLE WITH TYCHO

An Ace Science Fiction Book/published by arrangement with
the author

PRINTING HISTORY
Ace edition / 1961
This printing / April 1983

ISBN: 0-441-82443-9

Ace Science Fiction Books are published by Charter Communications, Inc.,
200 Madison Avenue, New York, N.Y. 10016.
PRINTED IN THE UNITED STATES OF AMERICA

THE TROUBLE WITH TYCHO

CHAPTER ONE

EVERYTHING was all right. Not making too much money, naturally. You very seldom do—unless you make that one big strike, and not many of us make it. But getting along well enough so that the syndicate was content to let their holdings ride. Not quite satisfied, of course, but let's give the kid a chance. They still think of me as a kid for all I'm twenty-seven.

Maybe I'd ought to explain about the syndicate. It has a big, hard sound to it, but it isn't really. It's just a bunch of people back in the old home town of Millville who put up some of their savings so that a Moon-struck kid they had watched grow up could go out there and try his luck. Not that I hadn't had to work on them plenty hard to talk them into it—that's understandable, for they're just small-town, average people, and conservative. There is Mel Adams, the banker, and Tony Jones, the barber, and Big Dan

1

Olson, who operates the drugstore, and a dozen or so others. I think the only reason they finally gave in was so they could talk about it. It isn't everyone who can say he has an investment on the Moon.

So there I was, rolling along in the rig and thinking about all the folks back home and glad that I was finally heading into Coonskin after four days spent Out Back. Don't ask me why they call it Coonskin, either, or why they call the place down by Schomberger, Crowbait, or that other settlement in Archimedes, Hungry Crack. You'd think they'd call these places by a lot of fancy names, like the names of all those scientists they named the craters for, or that at least they'd be called Lunarville or Moontown or some other name that made some sort of sense. But I guess that's just the way it goes. In those days when the Moon was a long ways off it was okay to hang all those high-sounding place-names on it, but when the people got there they picked old familiar names that had a homely sting to them.

I had spent my four days out northwest of Tycho and it was a crazy place—all the land stood up on end —but I hadn't done too badly. I had a fair-sized bag of lichens stuffed in the refrigerator and the quick test I had run on them showed that they crawled with microbes.

I was getting close to Pictet, less than an hour from home, when I saw the other rig. I was coming down a hogback that rimmed one edge of a little sawed-off swale when I caught the gleam, sitting at the edge of shadow. I kept an eye fastened on the gleam, wondering if it might be a glass outcropping. There's a lot of volcanic glass around. That's what the rays are made of mostly, and the finest ray system on the Moon is in the Tycho region.

I don't know what it was that kept me watching, but there must have been something about it that helped me to get my wind up. After you've lived on the Moon for a couple of years or so, you get a feeling for it. Screwy as its landscape is, you get familiar with it; you get a sort of blueprint of it fixed inside your skull. And the upshot of it is that, without knowing why, you can spot something instantly that is out of character. Back on Earth you'd call it woodcraft, but that's sure the wrong word here.

I wheeled my rig around and headed down the hogback, pointing for the gleam. Susie, my hound dog, came up out of the radio, where she had been resting, or hiding, or whatever Susie did. She perched on the rim of the wheel and fluttered in excitement and sparks flew out of her. At least they looked like sparks. They really weren't sparks.

A meteorite pinged somewhere on the rig. It scared the hell out of me. It scares you every time—not the sound so much as the sudden realization that it might have been a big one and that would have been the end. This one probably wasn't bigger that a millimeter—a good-sized grain of sand. But it was traveling several miles a second and it packed a lot of punch.

I reached the foot of the hogback and went bowling across the floor of the small depression, and now I saw the gleam came from a moon-rig. It wasn't moving, and there was no one near that I could see. It looked like it had been parked, and if someone had parked it out there in the sun with the shadow not to distant, they either were stark crazy or a terrible greenhorn. When you park your rig during the lunar day you always try to park it in the shade.

The Moon gets hot, let no one tell you different. Not as hot here in the polar regions as it gets in the equatorial zone, but plenty hot enough—up to 250° centigrade in the afternoon. You have your refrigerating units, sure, but they cost a lot of power to run and there are two things that are precious on the Moon—power and oxygen. You hoard them like a miser. Not because you are short on power, because the atomics pack a lot of power. But you are never long on water, and you have to hoard the water to drive the steam turbine.

I swung the rig up close, shutting off the turbine. I flipped my helmet over my head and heard it click, slapped the top of it to get it firmly seated. When you're out on the surface, even in a rig, you always wear your spacesuit. Then, if a meteorite should smash the rig without killing you, or should punch a big hole in it, you have a second chance. Although, truth to tell, that second chance isn't worth too much to a lone man stranded miles from nowhere in nothing but a spacesuit.

I opened the door that led into the lock. Once inside, I pushed the lever that shut the inner door, then opened the outer one. I crawled out, like a worm wriggling from an apple. It's not too dignified, but the principle of the engineering is sound and that counts for a lot. Dignity doesn't count for much out here on the Moon.

As soon as I stuck my head out, I was blinded by the glare. I had forgotton to put down the filter visor. You don't need it when you're in the cab, for the visiplate has a filter of its own. I cussed myself, not because I had caught the glare, but for forgetting. You don't forget, even minor things, and stay alive for long.

I couldn't reach the visor, for my arms were trapped at my side and I had to wiggle clear before I could pull down the visor. So I squeezed my eyes tight shut until I could get my hands free.

The first thing I saw was that the outer door of the parked rig's hatch stood open, so I knew that whoever had been in it had gotten out. I felt a little silly for the momentary alarm that I had felt. Although in coming up I had only done what might have been expected. You don't meet to many people when you're out, and it's just plain good manners to stop by and say hello.

I walked toward the rig, and not until then did I

see the neat round hole drilled through the visiplate.

I turned up the volume on my suit radio: "Is there anybody here?"

There wasn't any answer. And Susie, who had come out with me, danced excitedly in front of me, twinkling and flashing. No matter what you say of them, there are times when the hound dogs are good company.

"Hello," I yelled again. "Do you need some help?"

Although that was a silly question. The meteorite must have slammed straight through the control panel and the rig was useless as it stood. A dime would have fitted almost exactly in the hole and that is big enough to make an awful mess.

A voice came faintly to me.

"Hello. You bet I need some help."

It was a funny voice. It sounded womanish.

"How bad is it?"

"Bad enough," said the voice. "Be with you in a minute. I was working at it, but it got too hot. I had to get into the shade."

I knew what it would be like inside the rig. With the refrigerating units off, it would heat up fast. With the sun beating down through all the glass, the hothouse effect would shove the temperature far above the surface heat.

"I can tow you into town," I said. "It's just an hour or so away."

"Oh, I can't do that. I can get it fixed."

A spacesuit-clad figure came around the rig and walked over to me.

"I'm Amelia Thompson," she said, holding out her hand.

I took the hand, the steel of our gloved fingers grating at the grip.

"A woman?"

"And why not?"

"No reason, I guess. There just aren't many of them out here. I've never heard of one before."

I couldn't see her face, for she had the filter down.

There was a hound dog riding on her shoulder. Susie drifted over and spun around the roosting thing. They shot sparks at one another.

"Perhaps," she said, "you could push it over in the shadow and let it cool a bit."

"Amelia," I told her, "my name is Chris Jackson and I'm no Samaritan, but I can't let you stay out here with that panel jury-rigged. And that's the best that you can do. It could go out on you a dozen times in the next thirty miles. You're simply asking for it."

I can't go back to town," she said.

"And I won't let you stay here. You're crazy to even think of it."

She motioned to my rig. "Do you mind?" she asked. "We could talk it over."

"Certainly," I told her, although for the life of me I couldn't figure what there was to be talked about.

We walked over to my rig and she went in ahead

of me. I waited for a minute and then went in myself.

I pulled the rig ahead, out of the sun.

The two hound dogs sat side by side upon the panel, sparkling very quietly.

Then I turned around.

She had flipped her helmet back and she was smiling at me, but in a determined sort of way. Her hair was black and straight, cut square across the front. She had milk-white skin and a lot of freckles. She looked like a schoolgirl who had suddenly decided to grow up.

I did the honers. I went to the refrigerator to get the water flask. I had to walk around her to get there. We didn't have much room. The cab of an exploration tractor isn't very big.

I got the flask and a couple of glasses. I poured a big one for her, a short one for myself. I figured that she needed it. After a few hours in a suit, with only a sip now and then of tepid water from the tube, you dream of ice-cold water.

She drank it thirstily and handed back the glass.

"Thank you," she said.

I filled it up again.

"You shouldn't have done that. It's pure extravagance."

I shook the flask. There was still some in it, but it was the last I had.

"Almost home," I told her. "I won't be needing it."

She sipped at the second glass, making it last. I

knew the kind of restraint it took for her not to gulp it down. There are times when your body screams for the cold and wet.

I put the flask back in the refrigerator. She saw the bag of lichens.

"Good trip," she said.

"Not too bad. Lousy with the microbes. Doc will be glad to get them. He's always running short."

"You sell them to the sanitarium?"

I nodded. "Keeps the outfit running while I hunt for other things."

"What other things?"

"The usual. Uranium. Chromite. Diamonds. Anything at all. I even pick up agates. Found some beauties last trip."

She laughed a short and throaty laugh. "Agates!"

"There's a fellow in Coonskin makes a hobby of them. Cuts and polishes them. Keeps what he likes, ships the rest to Earth. Good steady demand for gem stones from the Moon. Don't have to be good. Just so they're from the Moon."

"He can't pay you much for them."

"He pays me nothing. He's a friend of mine. He does me little favors."

"I see," she said.

She was looking at me with a calculating squint, as if she might be making up her mind.

She finished off the water and handed back the glass.

"There's another left," I offered.

She shook her head.

"Chris," she said, "would you mind just going on to town and forgetting that you saw me. You could push the crate into the shadow for me. I'll get along."

I shook my head. "No soap. You'd be committing suicide. I can't let you do it."

"I can't go back to Coonskin—"

"You can't stay here," I said.

"I can't go back to Coonskin because I'm illegal. I haven't got a license."

"So *that's* it," I said.

"You make it sound pretty nasty."

"Not that. It just isn't very smart. You know what a license is for—so they can keep tabs on you. So that if you get into a jam—"

"I won't get into a jam."

"Your in a jam right now," I told her.

"I can get out of it."

I felt like belting her, just to snap her out of it.

She was putting me in an impossible position. I couldn't let her go on with the panel jury-rigged, and I couldn't turn her in. There's just one rule Out Back. Us prospectors stick together. You help another fellow anyway you can. You never snitch on him.

The time will come, perhaps in another hundred years or so, when there are too many of us, when we'll steal from and lie about and rat on one another —but that time is not yet.

10

"I could help you rig it up," I told her, "but that is not the point. You're taking your life in your hands if you go on with it that way. You need a complete replacement job. And there's that hole punched in the plate."

"I can patch that up."

And she was right, she could.

She said, "I have to get to Tycho. I simply have to get there."

"Tycho!"

"Yes. You know the crater."

"No Tycho!" I said, a little horrified.

"I know," she said. "A lot of silly stories."

She didn't know what she was talking about. The stories weren't silly. They were hard, cold record. They were down in writing. Men still living in Coonskin remembered what had happened.

"I like your looks," she said. "You're an honest man."

"The hell with that," I said.

I went over to the controls and started up the engine.

"What are you doing now?"

"I'm going to Coonskin."

"You're going to turn me in."

"No," I said. "I'm going to turn you over to this agate-loving friend of mine. He'll hide you out until we figure what to do. And keep away from that hatch. I'll swat your fanny if you make a dive for it."

For a moment I didn't know if she was going to cry or jump me like a wildcat. It turned out that she did neither.

"Wait a minute," she said.

"Yes?"

"You ever heard of the Third Lunar Expedition?"

I nodded. Everyone had heard of it. Two ships and eleven men swallowed by the Moon—just dropping out of sight. Thirty years ago and they never had been found.

"I know where it is," she said.

"Tycho?"

She nodded.

"So what?"

"So there are papers there."

"Papers . . ."

Then it hit me. "You mean museum stuff!"

"You can imagine what it's worth."

"And the story rights. '(I Found the Lost Lunar Expedition).' "

She nodded. "They'd make a book of it, and a movie, and it would be on television."

"And the government maybe would pin a medal on you."

She said, "After. Not before."

I saw what she meant. Open your yap up now and they'd push you to one side and go storming out, stories or no stories, to collect the glory for themselves.

Amelia Thompson looked at me again with that calculating stare.

"You've got me across a barrel," she said. "I'll make it fifty-fifty."

"That's right," I said. "Share and share alike. Both of us stone dead. They tried to build an observatory there. They had to give it up."

She sat silently, looking around the cab. It was a small place. There wasn't much to see.

"How big a mortgage do you have on this?" she asked.

I told her a hundred thousand dollars.

"And someday the syndicate will get tired of carrying you," she said, "and they will sell you out."

"I would think it quite unlikely," I told her, but I wasn't nearly as confident as I tried to make it sound. Even as I answered, I could see them drinking coffee at the drugstore, or setting around and talking in the barbershop, or maybe taking off their jackets and settling down to an evening of poker in the back room at the bank. And I knew just how easy it would be for them to idly talk themselves into dissatisfaction first and into panic later.

"Right now," she said, "you're just barely managing to get by. You're always hoping for that lucky strike. How many have you known who hit that lucky strike?"

I had to say, "Not many."

"Well, this is it," she said. "Here is your lucky strike. I'm offering it to you."

"Because," I reminded her, "you are across a barrel."

She smiled a bit lopsidely.

"That and something else."

I waited.

"Maybe it's because it's not a one-girl job. I tell you, mister, honestly, I was scared half to death before you came rolling up."

"You thought at one time it was a one-girl job?"

"I guess I did," she said. "You see, I had a partner. Then he flunked out on me."

"Let me guess," I said. "His name was Buddy Thompson. Where is Buddy now?"

For I suddenly remembered him. He'd operated out of Coonskin a year or so before. He'd been around for a month or so and then he had wandered off. It's not too many prospectors who stick to one place for long.

"Buddy is my brother. He ran into tough luck. He got caught in a radiation storm and was too far from cover. He's in the hospital up at Crowbait."

"That's tough," I said, and really meant it. It was the kind of thing that could happen to any man without a second's notice. That was one of the reasons you didn't go wandering around out in the open too far from your rig. And even with your rig nearby you kept a weather eye out for caves or walls or crevasses that were in handy reach.

"He'll be all right," Amelia said, "but it will take a while. They may have to send him back to Earth for better treatment."

"That will cost a pile of money."

"More than we've got," she said.

"And you came from Crowbait."

"I was flown in, rig and all," she said. "That took about the last cash that I had. I might have made it on the ground, but it's pretty far."

"Pretty chancey, too."

"I had it planned," she said, and I could see her getting sore at the way it had worked out. "This flier brought me in and put me on the spaceport. I drove over to the administration building and parked off to one side. I walked into the building as if I were heading for the registration desk, but I didn't go there. I went to the powder room and waited there almost an hour until I heard a ship come in. Then I walked out and everyone was busy and no one noticed me. I walked over to the rig and simply drove away."

"Crowbait will notify—"

"Oh, sure, I know," she said. "But by that time it'll be too late. I'll either have what I'm going after or there'll be no more Amelia Thompson."

I sat there, thinking of the sheer impudence of what she'd got away with. Since she was working in Coonskin jurisdiction, she would have had to have a Coonskin license so that Coonskin Central could keep track of her. She would have had to file a travel plan, and report in by radio every twenty hours. Let her fail to do so and the rescue units would be out. And a setup such as that would have cramped her style.

Anyhow, they wouldn't have given her clearance for Tycho. They probably would have grabbed her rig if she'd even breathed the word. Tycho was pure poison and everybody knew it.

So she'd landed on the strip and gone to the office so that anyone seeing her would figure she'd gone to get her license and file her travel plan. And when she came out again, if anyone had noticed her, they would have figured that she had her license and wouldn't give the matter any thought at all.

And that way, without any license, without a travel plan, with not a line of record except back at Crowbait, she was perfectly free to go anywhere she wished.

It was, I told myself, a swell suicidal setup.

"Buddy found the man," she said, "on the outer slopes of Tycho."

"What man?"

"One of the Lunar Three crew. He'd got away somehow, from whatever had happened. His name was Roy Newman."

"Buddy should have reported it."

"Of course, I know he should have. He knew it too.

But I ask you, what would you have done? Our time was running out, our money running low. There are times when you have to take a gamble—even with the law."

She was right. There were times when you had to take a gamble. There were times when you got desperate. There were times when you said the hell with it and risked everything you had.

Usually you lost.

"This Newman had a diary. Not too well kept, as it turned out. But it told how they'd all made out their wills and written out their stories—"

"Those are the papers you're after?"

She nodded.

"But you couldn't keep those papers. They'd have to go back to the families."

"Yes, I know," she said. "But we could photostat them, and we'd have the story and the story rights. And there'd be other papers, ones that weren't personal. There are other things besides. That expedition had a lot of scientific instruments. And there are the ships. There were two of them, one of them a passenger, the other one a cargo. Can you imagine what those two ships would be worth today?"

"But they aren't—"

"Yes, they are," she said. "They're salvage. I looked it up. The limitation has run out. It's finders keepers now."

I thought about it and it was a mint of money. Even

after thirty years those ships might still be serviceable, if meteors hadn't punched them full of holes. And even if they weren't they'd bring a good scrap price. Fabricated metal, right here on the Moon, would be worth a lot of money.

"Look," she said. "Let's get down to business. You could leave me here. You could hurry back with a replacement panel. We could do this together. They know you back in Coonskin. You could file a travel plan for the outer slopes of Tycho. You could get away with it. We could get that far without them checking up on us."

I sat there thinking and there was nothing wrong with it except that you were throwing the rules back into their faces. If you found this expedition you would be a hero, and maybe rich to boot. And if you failed, you'd probably be dead and it wouldn't matter to you.

I thought of the years behind me and of the years ahead and I imagined the members of the syndicate sitting in the barbershop, snapping their suspenders. And I imagined how good it would feel to walk down Millville's streets again and have all the people say, *There goes Chris Jackson. He made it on the Moon.*

"Fifty-fifty," Amelia Thompson said.

"Let's split it into thirds," I said. "We can't deal Buddy out."

That's the trouble with me—I have a sentimental streak.

CHAPTER TWO

WE HAD six days of light to do it, and by the time I got back that margin would be cut to something less than five. But in five days a man can do a lot. From where Amelia's rig stood, it was only a few hours time to the rim of Tycho.

We could come back in the dark—if we were coming back—but we needed light to do the job itself.

I drove mechanically, thinking as I drove, alternately damning myself as a fat-headed fool for touching any of my good luck to pick up such a deal.

And scared. I was scared pink, with purple spots.

Because, no matter what Amelia said, Tycho wasn't anything for a man to fool around with. Just what was there no man pretended to know, but some of the speculations were enough to curl the short hairs on your neck.

They had wanted, in the early days, some twenty years ago, to build an astronomical observatory on the floor of Tycho, but after what had happened they built it in Cuvier instead. They had sent out a surveying crew to lay out the Tycho installation and the crew had disappeared. A land rescue crew went out and the rescue crew evaporated, as it were, not into thin air, but rather into space. Space search went out and the ships shot across the crater, crisscrossing it for hours. The crater was empty of all life. There was not a single movement nor any hint of it. The surveying instruments stood where the men had left them. Bundles and piles of other equipment and supplies lay darkly about. There were tracks that led southward, but they seemed to end in the blankness of the crater wall. There was no sign of men.

That was the end of it. No one else went into the crater or even close to it. You sort of went stiff-legged circling cautiously when you came in miles of it. No one in his right mind would consider going down into the crater.

I don't suppose I was strictly of sound mind.

Let's cut out the fooling and be honest. No Moon prospector is ever of sound mind. If he had a brain at all he would be safely back on Earth.

Susie perched on the panel and she wasn't sparkling much. I could see she was depressed. The radiation counter kept up a steady clicking. The dead white of the gully running between two walls spun out like a railroad track before me, and I was pouring on the coal. I had left most of my oxygen with Amelia and I had no time to waste. Run out of oxygen and you've had it. You can only hold your breath so long.

And I was worrying, not only about the oxygen, but about Amelia, too. Although I suppose I shouldn't have, for she seemed to be a level-headed kid. She had oxygen enough; I'd pushed her rig into the shade and that shade would hold until the dawn of another lunar day. Except for the thermal units in her suit, she'd have no heat, of course, but anytime she got cold all she had to do was step out in the sun and she'd get warmed up. We'd plugged the hole in the visiplate so she could live in the cabin of the rig and she had plenty of water.

Directly south of me loomed the broken western wall of Pictet, and to the southwest the more distant peaks of Tycho, glistening spears of white thrust into the coal-black sky.

There was dust in the gully bottom and that was not so good. You never knew the minute when you might hit a hole hidden by the dust. It might be just a little hole or it might be big enough to swallow you and a dozen other rigs.

But I didn't have the time to start hunting around for a safer rubble surface. And I didn't have the time to creep along at a slow and cautious pace that would have allowed me to brake the machine and back it up to safety if I had hit a hole.

If I had known that the gully had been dust, I never would have gotten into it; but the upper reaches of it, where the walls were lower, had been sound and solid gravel and very easy going. I could see ahead, of course, but in the white glare of the sun there is no telling at a distance the difference between dust and gravel.

That's the one thing that hits you about the Moon when you first step off the spaceship. The Moon is black and white. Except for the streaks of color here and there in some rock formation, there isn't any color. And you only see that color when you are near by. The glare of the sun whitewashes everything. And where there is no sun, there is utter blackness.

So I went bowling down that dust alley—dust that had never known a track before; dust all pitted by tiny one-inch craters pinged out by the whizzing bits of debris that come storming in from space; dust that had piled up for ages, chiseled off the walls by the endless hammering of the radiations, by the clicking bits of sand moving miles a second, by the slow patience of the heat and cold that spanned hundreds of degrees.

It's a mean life and a bitter one and hard, but there's a lot of glory and of beauty in the very harshness of the Moon. She is waiting for a slip to kill you, she has no mercy in her, she simply doesn't give a damn; but there are times when she can cut your breath with the very wonder of her, when she can take your soul and lift it high into the black emptiness of space and give you peace and insight. And there are other times when she simply strikes you numb.

That's the way she had me now, sitting stiff and rigid, with my throat bone-dry and the fine sweat standing out, whooping down that alley where a trap might wait me and not a chance to dodge it.

I made it. My number just didn't happen to be up that time. Old Madam Moon had saved me for another day.

I came out of the gully onto a flat, smooth plain a couple of miles across. Just beyond the plain was Hunkadory pass that led into Pictet and Coonskin.

The terrain was rubble now and it was good going. I took a look at the cab's oxygen supply and the needle was swinging close down toward the pin, but I had enough. Even if I didn't, I still had a little in the tank on my suit and I would be all right.

So I'd come through the dust all right and the oxy looked about to last and there was very little to worry about right then.

I drove up the short slope of the pass and there was Pictet spread out before me, a ringed plain with the town of Coonskin huddled against the northeast wall; and out beyond the town the sharp, hard glitter of the spaceport, which was used as a staging center for the other planets. Even as I watched, a spaceship came mushing down on it with the mushrooming flame of barking jets spewing down with a firey viciousness. And it was weird to watch it, for all the power, all that ferocity of flame, was blanked by utter silence.

The whiteness and the blackness of the Moon is what first impresses you, but it is the terrible arrogance of its silence that lives with you all the days you spend upon its surface. The silence is the one thing, the one unbelievable and unacceptable thing that is very hard to live with.

I picked my way slowly down the pass, for there was little more than a trail and there were some turns that called for creeping speed. The oxygen needle swept lower, but I knew that I was safe.

I reached the bottom of the slope and turned to my left. I went around a talus slope that bulged out from the ringwall, and there, huddled in the angle between the slope and the wall itself, was the sanitarium.

On the Moon you don't build out in the open. You build against high walls, you huddle under mountains, you look for little nooks, for you need protection. You need protection from the radiation and the meteorites. You can't get complete protection except by going underground, and there's something in the human make-up that rebels against living out one's life in burrows. But you can get shielding of a sort by building in the angel of high walls, and that was the way of Coonskin. It was strung out for almost three miles, with no streets at all, but all the buildings standing against the high north wall.

I pulled around and stopped outside the sanitarium lock. I slapped down my helmet and took the bag of lichens and crawled out of the rig. Someone inside the sanitarium must have seen me, for the outer lock was beginning to unscrew. By the time I got there it had whirled free and dropped back, and I stepped into the chamber. The outer lock closed behind me, and I heard the hiss of air being fed into the chamber. I waited for the inner lock to open; then I unhinged my helmet and stepped into the building.

Doc Withers was waiting there for me and he grinned beneath his great, gray walrus mustache when he saw the bag I carried.

"Katie," he called, and then he was reaching for the bag with one hand and thumping my shoulder with the other.

"We need that stuff," he said. "We're running low. None of the other boys had been in since it got light. You are the first of them."

He sucked in his breath and blew it out in a lengthy gust. "I always worry," he declared, "that they all will make good strikes and then no one will bother to hunt my precious little microbes."

"Not much chance of that," I said.

Katie made her appearance. She was a rugged old fossil, with the pinched, bleak face of a nurse who has been too long on duty, who has absorbed too great a penchant for authority, has become passionately devoted to her profession of caring for the sick.

Doc handed her the bag.

"Run a test and weigh it up," he said. "I'm glad that some came in."

Katie took the bag. She turned a bleak look on me.

"Why did you take so long?" she asked, as if it were all my fault. "We're running short of it."

She went back down the corridor.

"Come on," invited Doc. "Crawl out of the armor and let us have a drink. You'll have to wait until Katie has it figured up."

"I'd better keep the suit," I said. "I would stink like hell."

"You can even have a bath," Doc offered.

"I'd better keep the suit."

"If it's the smell, I've worked in hospitals all my life—"

"I'll be home in a little while," I told him. I'll take the suit off then. But I could stand the drink."

Doc led the way into his office. It was small, but it was a comfortable-looking place. It's hard to make a room—any room—on the Moon look comfortable. It's hard to soften metal walls and floors and ceilings. You can paste up pictures on the walls, you can cover them with drapes, you can even paint them in pastels—the steel will show through. You can sense and feel and taste it. You can never forget the coldness and the hardness of it. And you never quite forget why it is steel instead of something else.

The illusion of comfort in Doc's office came from the soft, deep furniture with which he'd filled the room. There were chairs and lounges that, when you sat in them, all but swallowed you.

Doc opened up a cupboard and got out a bottle and some glasses. He even had some ice. I knew it would be good stuff. There's no poor liquor on the Moon—or anywhere else in space. The freight charges are so high that there isn't any sense in trying to save a dollar or two on a fifth.

"A good trip?" asked Doc.

"I picked up a fair amount of lichens. Nothing else."

"I live in mortal dread," said Doc, "that the day will come when there will be no more. We have tried to grow them under artificial conditions—artificial, but theoretically ideal—and they simply will not grow. We have tried to transplant them to places of our own choosing right here on the Moon, and we've been sucessful. We've sent them to Earth, and they've had no luck at all. It appears they cannot tolerate even the faintest shred of atmosphere."

He went on fixing the drinks.

"There may be other places on the Moon where they can be found," I said.

Doc shook his head. "The only place they ever have been found is in the Tycho region."

Susie had come in with me and now she perched

on top of the whiskey bottle. I don't know if she's a potential toper, but she gets an awful kick out of liquor bottles.

"Cunning little cuss," Doc said, nodding his head at her.

He handed me the drink. I took a taste of it. It was exactly what I needed. It cut the nonexistent dust out of my throat, it took the slimy feeling right out of my mouth. I took a good gulp of it.

"The two of them seem to go together, Doc—the hound dogs and the lichens. You don't find one unless you find the other. There are always a few hound dogs hanging around a bunch of lichens. Like butterflies hang around a row of flowers. That little Susie there is the best little lichen hunter I've ever seen."

I took another long swallow, and I thought about how the hound dogs and the lichens and the microbes were all bound up together. It sure was a screwy thing. The hound dogs found the lichens, and the lichens had the microbes, and it was, of course, the microbes that Man actually was hunting. It was the microbes that he used.

But that wasn't it—that wasn't all of it.

"Doc," I said, "you and I—we're good friends, aren't we?"

"Why, I guess we are," said Doc. "Yes, my boy, I'd say there was no question about it."

"Well, I have a funny feeling. Two funny feelings,

really. The first of them is that sometimes Susie tries to talk to me."

"Nothing too funny about that," said Doc. "We don't know a thing about her or any of her tribe. She could be intelligent. I would make a guess she was. She seems to be pure energy, although no one knows for sure. There is nothing that says that to be intelligent you've got to be made of hide and bone and muscle."

"And there are other times," I said, "when it seems to me she might be studying me. Not me alone, you understand, but the human race. Maybe I tell myself, that's why she picked me up—so she could study me."

Doc lowered himself pondersouly into a chair so that he sat facing me.

"You wouldn't have told this to anyone but a real good friend," he said.

I shook my head. I wondered why I'd told even him. I had never breathed it to a soul before. "Anyone else might think I was nuts," I said.

"Not that," he told me. "There is no one, absolutely no one, who knows about the Moon. We've just scratched the surface of it."

"I remember when I was a boy people used to wonder why we should bother going to the Moon. There was nothing there, they said. Nothing that was worth the going. They said that even if there was it would cost too much to ship it back. They said the Moon was just another chunk of Earth, but a mighty poor chunk, without any life and without any atmosphere and without much of anything. Whoever would have thought, of all things, that in this utterly worthless place we would find one of the things for which man had searched so long—a cure for mental illness."

I nodded. If Doc wanted to talk, I was perfectly willing to let him talk. I didn't have a thing to do except to get back to Amelia, who was stuck out in the wilderness with a busted panel. And I was all beat out. All I wanted to do was just sit there. I took another hefty drink. Doc reached out and filled the glass. I didn't try to stop him.

"We need more space in this sanitarium," said Doc, "and money is no problem. We could find the cash to enlarge it three times over, but what would be the sense of it? We barely get enough of the lichens to handle the cases that we have."

"Raise the price," I told him. "The boys will hunt the harder. They'll give up the foolishness of looking for uranium and diamonds and other junk like that."

Doc looked at me sharply. "I suppose you're joking. I am worried, Chris."

"There will be other places found where the lichens grow," I said. "There are only five settlements on the Moon so far. Three here and two up at the North Pole. By and large, the Moon's not been explored. There have been some low-level camera runs, of course, and a few land traverses, but there are many places Man has never seen. There are huge areas where he's never set foot."

Doc shook his head. "No, I don't believe it. There's something funny about the lichen situation. I've thought about it a lot and it's haunted me. There is no apparent reason why the lichens should grow only in the Tycho region, unless. . ."

"Unless what?" I asked, but I didn't wait for him to answer the question.

"Unless there's something in Tycho," I said. "Unless the lichens originated in Tycho and are spreading out from it."

Doc sat there staring at me, not taking his eyes off me.

"What's in Tycho, Chris? You prowl around a lot out there. Have you seen anything?"

"Never close enough," I told him.

"Some day," said Doc, "someone will find out. Someone with lots of guts. Some day someone will say to hell with all the superstitions and go down and have a look."

Katie came in just then with a slip of paper and handed it to Doc. She sneered at me and left.

Doc looked at the paper. "It figures out to a hundred seventy-five," he said. "Is that all right with you?"

"Anything you say," I told him.

You could say this for Doc—he was a square-shooter. You never had to question what he told you. He paid you every cent that was coming to you.

He dug his wallet out of his hip pocket and counted out the bills. He handed them across.

"Finish up your drink," he said, "and have another one."

"Can't take the time. I've got to hurry. Lots of things to do."

"You're going out again?"

I nodded.

"You'll keep a watch for lichens?"

"Sure. I always do. I could get a lot for you if I only could stay out. This business of not being able to keep them for more than a hundred hours or so makes it a little rough."

"I know," said Doc. "And if I could only bottle up the stuff and ship it back to Earth. . . Maybe someone some day will figure out a way. I've got sixty patients here—that's all the room I've got, that's all the lichens I have. There are reservations for three years ahead. People who are waiting to come out to the Moon so that we can cure them."

"Maybe someone can synthesize—"

He laughed a little harshly. "Have you ever seen a diagram of some of the molecules involved?"

"No," I said, "I never have."

"It can't be done," said Doc.

I tucked the bills in the pocket of my suit and set the glass on his desk.

I stood up. "Thanks for the drink," I said.

Susie came from wherever she had been roosting and whizzed around my head a couple of times. She shot out a bunch of sparks.

I said good-by to Doc and went out through the lock and got into the rig.

The spaceship I had seen coming in was sitting on the field and the field crew was hauling in the freight she carried. Apparently the passengers already had been taken off.

I kicked the turbine into life and headed for Sloppy Joe's—which definitely is not what you think it is, a little hamburger and chili joint. It's the biggest and almost the only business house in Coonskin. It has been around as long as Coonskin has. Joe started out in business when the spaceport was built. He housed and fed the construction crews, and because they loved the man himself, because they wanted to make the Moon seem as much like Main Street as possible, they called the place he kept for them Sloppy Joe's. And it's stayed that way ever since.

I pulled up in front of Joe's and parked the rig and went into the place.

It was like coming home. In fact, it was my home. There were a dozen or so of us who kept regular rooms at Joe's and we spent all our time there when we weren't roaming. For Joe's is quite a place by now. It's a sort of combination hotel-bar-bank-general store.

I came into the lobby and headed for the bar. Not so much because I needed a drink as I wanted to see who might be around.

As it turned out, there was hardly anybody. There was Tubby behind the bar and there was this other fellow standing at the bar, drinking.

"Hi, Chris," said Tubby. "Here's someone wants to see you."

The man turned around. He was a big man and a rough-looking customer, with shoulders that were so heavy they bent forward, as if at any moment they might fall off of him. He had great jowls with gray whiskers—not a beard, but just unshaven whiskers—and his eyes were blue as big-lake ice.

"You Jackson?" he demanded.

I admitted that I was.

"He came in on the ship less than an hour ago," said Tubby.

"My name is Chandler Brill," the big man said. I'm from Johns Hopkins back on Earth. I'm your new boss, but we'll get along all right."

He stuck out a hand that was bigger than mine even with my space glove on.

We shook. And there were cold shivers crawling up my spine.

"You mean that you bought out . . ."

"No, not that," said Brill. "I rented you and your outfit from the folks in Millville. I don't mind telling you they set a good high figure."

He reached into his pocket and handed me an envelope. "Here's a letter from them."

I took it and doubled it up and stuck it in my pocket.

I said, "I imagine you'll want a little time to get shook down before going out."

"Not at all," said Brill. "I can leave as soon as you're ready."

"What are we looking for?"

"Oh, different things. I'm a scientist of sorts."

"Here's your drink," Tubby said to me.

I moved up to the bar and picked up the drink and there were a million wheels, all moving madly, buzzing in my head.

I had to get this guy sidetracked somehow. I could fool around with him and leave Amelia stranded out there with a busted rig. No matter how crazy she might be, she was depending on me. And there was the matter, too, of the foray into Tycho. It was something that twenty hours before I would have sworn I'd never be fool enough, or have the guts, to do. But Doc had said that some day someone would say to hell with all the silly superstitions and all the crazy stories. Although they weren't silly and they weren't crazy; a lot of men had disappeared into the maw of Tycho.

"You got a lot of gear?" I asked of Brill.

"Almost none at all," he told me. "I've roughed it all over Earth. I know how to get along."

35

I nodded. "You'll be all right," I said.

I'd had an wild idea for a moment of discouraging him by a beef about a lot of gear, telling him that we couldn't take it, that sort wouldn't work with him. He didn't look like any scientist I had ever seen; he didn't even especially look like he had any sense at all. He looked just like a roughneck.

"How come Mel Adams didn't send me a radiogram?" I asked.

"Well," said Brill, "I was coming out immediately. Left as soon as I closed the deal with them. Adams gave me the letter, let me carry it. He's a thrifty man."

"Yeah, I know," I said.

"He didn't see the need of radioing. Said you'd probably be Out Back."

"They'd have radioed me the message from the port. I could have gotten back in time to meet you."

"Ah, well," said Brill, "let's not quibble now. Nothing has been hurt. How about us having something to eat?"

"I have to take a bath and get some clothes," I told him. "Soon as I do that I'll come down."

"I'll be waiting for you," said Brill.

"Tubby," I said, "give me that bottle over there."

Tubby handed me the bottle and I took it by the neck and started for the door.

"Hey," yelled Tubby, "you forgot the glass."

"I won't need no glass," I told him.

THE TROUBLE WITH TYCHO

If ever a man had an excuse to get roaring, sodden drunk, I told myself, that man was me.

CHAPTER THREE

I FILLED the bathtub almost to the top. Here in Coonskin we don't need to worry much about water. We've got plenty of it. There are cubic miles of ice located under Pictet and we have a mine that traps it. That's one of the reasons Coonskin grew up in Pictet instead of somewhere else. One of the earliest traverse parties ran a drill down into a crevasse underneath the north wall and hit this mass of ice.

Of course, Out Back you've got to be careful of your water, for you can't carry too much of it. But here in Coonskin you can simply wallow in it.

So I crawled out of my suit and hung it in the room's escape port and cracked the outer lock so that the suit could get aired out. Not aired out really—spaced out. Then I filled the tub with water and got a bar of soap and put the bottle down beside the tub within easy reach and settled down to soak.

Four days in a spacesuit can get you pretty high. You can't live with yourself. You're a stinking mess.

I lay there soaking, looking up at the ceiling; the ceiling was gray steel, like everything in Coonskin. And I thought what a rotten way to live, without a breath of fresh air, without a blade of grass, with no color, with no rosey dawn and no flaming sunset, without any rain or dew—without a single thing to make life a little better than a bare existence.

To brighten up the outlook just a bit, I hoisted up the bottle and had a healthy slug. But I decided that maybe I wouldn't get stinking drunk after all. There was too much to do and no time to do it in.

Susie came and sat on the hot water tap. I don't suppose she sat. It just looked like she was sitting. And don't ask me why I call her *she*. I don't suppose she actually is a she. A contraption like Susie isn't anything at all. It's just an it.

I offered her a drink and she bent into a shape like a question mark, with one end of her still on the tap and her nose of sparks into the bottle and pulled herself back into a lump of brilliance squatting on the tap. For a minute, before the sparks died out, that bottle was the prettiest thing you ever laid your eyes on. I was almost scared to drink out of it, but the sparks didn't seem to hurt the liquor any.

Then I remembered something that I should have done before, so I got out of the tub and went to the phone and called Herbie Grayle.

Herbie was the fellow I brought in the agates for. He worked down at Coonskin Central and they let him have the corner of the shop for his lapidary outfit. He had a diamond saw and a trimmer and a polisher and grinders and buffers and all the other stuff. He could take a piece of rock and make it into something that would knock your eyes out.

Herbie lived in a trailer that he had parked under an overhang, one of the safest places in all of Coonskin, and every week or so he had some of the boys over for a hand or two of poker. Herbie is a bachelor— I guess he's the only bachelor in Coonskin who lives in a trailer. All the other trailer people are married and some of them even have a kid or two.

Talk about a lousy place to raise a batch of kids!

Herbie was at home.

"Favor to ask of you," I told him.

"Go ahead," he said.

"I have a fellow downstairs the syndicate sent out. I've got to haul him around Out Back for a day or two."

"Tourist?"

"No. A scientist, he says."

"I suppose you'll want my trailer."

"If you don't mind," I said. "You could stay here in my room until I got back. It's paid for whether I use it or not."

"You might as well take the trailer," Herbie said. "Everybody borrows it when they have to haul some outsider into the wilderness."

"Thanks, Herbie," I said.

"Don't mention it," said Herbie.

"It gets a little crowded," I said. "Two men in a cab."

And I was figuring how I could park Brill somewhere in the trailer and tell him I was going off for an hour or two. There wasn't much that he could do about it if I didn't come back for a day or two and I could always cook up some sort of story about the bad luck I had had. He might not believe me, but that was not the point. All I needed was a cover for Coonskin Central. It might scare him spotted, but it wouldn't hurt him any. There would be plenty of food and air and water, and if something really happened and I wasn't coming back, Central would start out to hunt us and they would find the trailer.

"When will you want the trailer, Chris?" asked Herbie.

"I don't want to hurry you."

"Any time," said Herbie.

"Let's say twelve hours. I want to get some sleep."

"I'll pack what I need and bring it over. I'll leave the rest just as it is."

"Thanks, Herbie."

"No need," said Herbie. "You've brought me lots of rocks."

I hung up and started back to the tub. Passing the dresser I saw the letter I'd pulled out of the pocket of my suit and thrown there.

I picked it up and got back into the tub. I began to soak again and I opened up the letter. It said:

Dear Chris:

We do not wish to make it appear that we are interfering in your work by accepting Dr. Brill's offer to employ you. But in view of the fact that your prospecting, to the moment, has not met with the spectacular results which you had hoped, all of us felt you might welcome this opportunity to earn some extra money. We have investigated Dr. Brill and can tell you that he is a professor at Johns Hopkins and highly regarded in scientific circles. Let me assure you that all of us still have faith in you and know that in time your venture will meet with all hoped-for success.

Best regards,
Melvin Adams

I dropped the letter on the floor and lay there in the tub, and was just a little sick—for I read between lines of that letter, friendly on its surface, the first seeds of doubt among the men of Millville.

And I knew that somehow or other I must show results and the time was not too long.

I was as neatly trapped as a man had ever been. There was no dodging now. I had to go to Tycho. I had to take the chance that there was treasure there and that I'd get back alive.

Even if I wanted to chicken out, I couldn't afford to now. For in another month or two the syndicate would start edging out, and the creditors would start moving in, and I'd lose the Moon forever.

I could see myself, a glamorous failure, trudging down the streets of Millville, glad to take any job I could—another man who'd not made it on the Moon.

I got out of the tub and got into some clothes.

I began laying out a timetable. I would eat and have a talk with Brill, then I'd get some sleep. After that I'd file my travel plan. Then I'd hook up the trailer and dump my scientist into it and we would be off. There was no time to waste.

I might have some trouble with the travel plans, for I would have to list the outer slopes of Tycho. That way I could make a final report from the very rim and after that it would be twenty hours before Coonskin Central would think of me again.

And in twenty hours Amelia and I would have found what we were after or, just as likely, like the others, we'd not be coming back.

I took a final drink and went downstairs, with Susie fluttering before me.

Brill was waiting for me and we went into the dining room and found a table. Susie roosted on the sugar bowl.

Brill made a motion toward her. "Quite a pal you have."

"Susie hunts the lichens for me," I told him. "When she finds them she does a sort of dance and I go and pick them off the rocks."

"Any special training?"

"None at all. The hound dogs have some strange affiliation with the lichens. Where you find the hound dogs—the wild hound dogs, that is—you're sure to find the lichens."

"But this Susie of yours. Did you buy her or—"

"No, she just picked me up. First trip out. She tagged along. She's been with me ever since."

"And the other prospectors? Do they also have—"

"Every one of them. In this area. This is, you know, the only place on the Moon where any life has been discovered."

"That's why I'm here," said Brill. "I want you to take me where I can observe and study both the lichens and the hound dogs."

"The slopes of Tycho."

He nodded idly. "The bartender was telling me some hair-raising tales of Tycho. He figures that it's haunted.

"That's the crater itself," I told him. "You're safe out on the slopes."

He glanced at me sharply. "You believe that stuff?" he asked.

"Sure I do," I said.

After we had finished eating and had said good night, I went in search of Sloppy Joe. I found him in his office, a most untidy place. The man was not so neat himself. He had egg from two months before still upon his necktie.

Yes, he told me, some money had come in. The syndicate, just hours before, had deposited by radio ten thousand dollars to my account.

"Payment for services you are to render to one Chandler Brill," he said. "I understand the gent is already in the house."

I said that I had met him.

"For that kind of money," said Sloppy Joe, "I hope you take excellent care of him."

I promised that I would.

I ordered a bunch of oxygen and quite a hunk of water and some other things, not forgetting the control panel for Amelia's rig. Sloppy Joe thought that was a great extravagance and tried to argue me out of buying it, but I told him I'd worried a lot about something happening to my panel. I said that a meteorite could knock it out of kilter at anytime, and he laughed his fool head off. I told him I'd heard of it happening once. Up at the North Pole, I said. And the fellow had to walk forty miles and he was lucky to be that close. Walking, I can tell you, is no picnic even in the lesser gravity.

Joe said that walking in was all damn foolishness; all you had to do was sit it out and the rescue crew would get you. I pointed out to him they fined you a thousand clams for getting in a jam so that you needed rescue. He said yes, that was true; he guessed a thousand bucks was good to middling pay for walking forty miles. He said that right away he'd have all the stuff delivered and stowed in Herbie's trailer.

He hauled a bottle out and we had a couple. Then I said good night to him and staggered off to bed.

CHAPTER FOUR

I came down across the hogback and I saw that the shadow had crept across the depression a short distance since I had left the place less than eighteen hours before. I looked across to the opposite hogback and I could see the wheel marks where I had come down to check on Amelia's rig.

So I was certain that I was in the right place and that is always something you must be absolutely sure of. The Moonscape has a lot of landmarks that you can't mistake, but there likewise are a lot of places that look exactly like a lot of other places. This is because there is so few natural features you lose certain dimensions for identifying places.

But this time I was sure. This was my own backyard. This one I could feel my way around in without even seeing it. And there were the wheel marks to cinch the matter absolutely.

I swung up the depression and any moment I expected to see a slight reflection from Amelia's rig. It was in the shadow because I had pushed it there and the creeping of the shadow had, since then, put it even farther back from the sunlight line. But even so, the edge of the shadow is not entirely black; there is enough reflection from the sunlit surfaces to give it a sort of twilight effect for some distance back from the fringes of it.

But I caught no glint of metal—not a thing at all. Just the hazy twilight that shaded into blackness, with the jagged outline of the hogback like the bristling hump of some prehistoric monster.

I drove past the place where I was sure Amelia's rig must be, and there was no sign of it. I nosed into the shadow and turned on my searchlight and the cone of brightness showed me nothing but the dreariness of pea-sized rubble and the flats of rock dust and little boiling areas where the dust, electrified by the inpouring solar radiation, hopped and jumped and skipped like a frying pan of fleas.

Undimmed and undiffused by any atmosphere, the beam stabbed straight and true, turning the dark to brightness, clear to the hogback's base. In that brilliance a rabbit couldn't have kept from being seen. I swiveled the light back and forth and there was nothing there.

I sat there, hunched in the seat, and the fact soaked in that Amelia wasn't there. It was hard to believe, and yet, somehow, it was no surprise. I sat there, sweating with fear that jingled through me, yet cold with bitter rage.

And this was it, I thought. This relieved me of all responsibility. If she wanted to take it on the lam as soon as I turned my back, that was up to her.

Now I could go back to where I left Brill and the trailer and tell him I'd figured out an easy route to Tycho and we could be on our way.

He had been a little huffy and slightly difficult when I had told him he'd have to stay with the trailer while I scouted out the land. It was a lie, of course, and he seemed to know it was, but he finally agreed. I pointed out to him there were a lot of places you couldn't take a trailer and that we'd save a lot of time and possible misadventure if I took a look ahead.

So I finally ditched him and had come on ahead to put the new control panel into Amelia's rig.

And now Amelia had gone off and left me and she could go to hell.

I switched off the searchlight and swung the rig around and went slowly down the edge of shadow toward the south end of the hogback.

I was sore at Amelia. I had a right to be. The little fool had jury-rigged the panel and had lit out for Tycho after I had warned her that it was worth her life to travel jury-rigged.

I reached the end of the hogback and stopped the

rig and sat there thinking. I knew just where she was. I knew what route she'd travel. There was only one decent route by which one could reach Tycho from this place.

And I couldn't let her do it. I couldn't live with myself if I let her do it. And I remembered, as well, the banker and the baker and the drugstore operator sitting back there in Millville, getting ready to jerk the rug right out from under me.

I started up the rig and swung it toward the southwest and poured on all the speed I could. I was pretty certain I could catch the little fool before she reached Tycho's rim. She couldn't have too great a head start on me; it would have taken quite a while to get the panel rigged and she'd have to have some sleep.

I was right about that. I caught up with her inside of ten miles, at the foot of a massive cliff that reared up out of a system of tangled craterlets just at the bottom of the huge upthrust of land that rose to Tycho's rim.

She had dug a hole in the cliff wall and was taking stuff out of the hole. She had cylinders of oxygen stacked up and was wrestling with a tin of water when I came storming around a curve and came up beside her rig.

From the way she dropped the water tin and jerked up her head, I could see that she was startled. She could not have heard me coming, for there's no sound on the Moon, and the ground was too rugged

52

for her to have caught sight of me.

I stopped the rig and got out of it as swiftly as I could.

I walked up to her and took in the situation.

"A cache," I said.

Her voice on the radio was rather small and frightened when she answered.

"My brother," she said. "He built it up in several trips. From going into Tycho."

"And I suppose," I said, "there's a panel replacement there as well as all this other stuff."

She said defensively, "It's working all right."

"Lady," I said, "where you're going there might not be time to jigger it again if it went out on you."

She got sore at me. "I was giving you an out," she yelled at me. "There is nothing that says you have to go along with me."

"And you've got over being scared?"

"Well, perhaps not entirely. But what has that to do with it?"

I went back to the rig and got the panel.

"Now let's get going on this," I told her, "and no more foolishness. I've got trouble enough without more shenanigans from you."

I told her about Brill and how we'd have to sneak away and leave him on the slope, all wrapped up in his hound dog and lichen chasing, while the two of us made our dash for Tycho.

"I'm sorry," she said. "Why don't you just bow

53

out? You could lose your license for a stunt like this."

"Not if we pull this Tycho business off."

We got the panel into her rig. I saw she had done a good job in patching up the visor.

"You're sure about Tycho?" I demanded.

"My brother found the body. And there was the diary."

"What did the diary say exactly?"

"Their radios went out while they were still in space. They still could use them, but no one apparently was receiving them. So they landed and tried to fix the radios, but it was no good. They either weren't getting through or there was something that was stopping their receiving. After a time they got scared and tried to take off and the rocket motors wouldn't work. Then something awful happened and—"

"What?"

"The diary didn't say. The man just wrote: 'I have to get out of here. I can't stand it any longer.' That was all there was to it."

"He went up the wall somewhere," I said. "He was running straight to death and he must have known it."

I wondered what he had been running from, but I didn't say it.

"So the spaceships still are there," I added, "and all those other men."

She looked at me and there was fright brimming in her eyes. "I don't know," she said.

We pulled out the old panel and got the new one bolted into place. I helped her get the oxygen and water stowed away. Some of it we had to lash in place on top of the rig. There wasn't room inside.

"You can finish the rest of it?" I asked.

"Without a bit of trouble. I know these circuits inside out."

"Okay, then," I told her. "When you get it all hooked up, take off. Get over the rim, but not too far. Sit there and wait for me. And maybe you should try to get a little sleep. It'll be a long hard drive down into the crater."

She stuck out a hand and we shook on it.

"No more tricks," I said.

"No more tricks. I'll be waiting just below the rim."

I crawled out of her rig and got into my own. I waved at her and she waved back; then I headed out of there, hurrying as fast as I dared back to the trailer and to Brill. I'd been gone for quite a while and he might be getting nervous.

He must have been watching for me and spotted me from a long ways off, for he had the coffee cooking and a bottle of brandy set out on the table when I crawled into the trailer.

"You were gone a while," he said.

"Had to do a lot of backtracking. Ran into a couple of dead ends."

"But you found a way."

I nodded.

He poured us cups of coffee and sloshed in liberal slugs of brandy.

"There's something I've been wanting to talk to you about," he said.

And here it comes, I thought. He was going to tell me that I was up to something and he knew it. He was all set to give me a real rough time.

"Shoot," I said, as casually as I could.

"You strike me as a man who's not too jittery," he said.

"You're jittery all the time," I said. "Everybody is. You never know, out here on the Moon . . ."

"What I mean is you seem to have some bravery."

"I'm not a coward. There are no cowards on the Moon."

"And a bit unscrupulous."

"Well, now that you mention it . . ."

"Not above the making of an extra dollar."

"Any time," I told him.

He picked up his coffee cup and drank most of what was in it at one fell swoop. He put it down again.

"How much would it need," he asked, "to persuade you to take me into Tycho?"

I choked on my coffee and slopped it all over the tabletop.

"You want to go into Tycho?"

"For a long time," said Brill, "I've had a sort of theory."

"Go ahead," I told him.

"Well, it's something you may have wondered at yourself. The lichens and the hounds . . ."

He quit and I sat looking at him.

"I'll make it worth your while," he said. "The syndicate need never know about it. This is something just between the two of us."

I pushed the coffee cup away and laid my arms down on the table and put my head down on them and I laughed. I thought I never would stop laughing.

CHAPTER FIVE

YOU STAND up on the rim and look down and there is Tycho, spread out like a map before you, wild and savage, raw and cold and hard, like the entryway to hell. The floor is pitted with little craters that, in some places, are so close together they overlap. There are rugged upheavels, and the soft, dreamlike plains that shimmer with the dancing dust, and the great jagged central mountain throwing a lop-sided shadow that is black as ink.

You look down and see the way that you must go to reach the crater floor and you would swear it was impossible except for the fact you know it can be done, since it has been done before. You see the tracks of the vehicles that have preceded you, cutting across the tiny talus slopes. The tracks are the same as when they were made twenty years ago, except for the tiny postmarks the meteorites have made, with here and there a broom-like smoothing out job done by the dancing dust motes, hopping about like jumping beans under the excitation of the solar wind.

And where these other rigs have gone you can be fairly sure that you can go as well, for the trial will be the same. Twenty years is no more than a second on the Moon, for there is no wind and weather and the erosion is minute—the erosion of the meteorites, of the solar wind, of the tiny hammerings of the heat and cold that may sliver a flake of debris from a rock once every hundred years.

There were three of us, I thought, who were going down there and each for a different reason, although Amelia and I, perhaps, had something in common.

Brill was going because he had the wild idea that down there in the crater he would find the answer to the lichens and the hound dogs—the only native life so far found upon the Moon. And perhaps his idea was not entirely wild, for it was only in Tycho region that one found the lichens and the hounds. It was entirely possible their origin was in Tycho and that those found outside the crater simply had slopped over.

Amelia was going down because she thought there was treasure to be found there—but even more than that she was an extension of a brother who could not carry on his quest, a brother for whom she needed money so he could go back to Earth for treatment of radiation sickness.

And I? I sought the treasure too. But something

more than treasure, although I could not at the moment put my finger on the nature of it.

And in going, all three of us were in defiance of the law.

Just a few minutes ago I had made my radio report back to Coonskin Central and now we had twenty hours before they could expect us to report again. And in those twenty hours, I wondered what would happen to us.

I craned my head around and saw Amelia's rig behind us.

I said to Brill, "Well, here we go, God help us."

I put in the clutch and the rig moved forward slowly, nosing down, rocking to the unevenness of the trail.

It was tricky driving. The curves and switchbacks were steep and tight, and at times the trail was little wider than the rig itself. Time after time the pressure of the outer wheels crumbled the edge of the trackway and sent fine dust and clods trickling down the slope below.

I clung to the wheel and my palms were sweating and I began a grim and bitter mental race with time. A thousand feet, I estimated, and eleven more to go. And then two thousand feet and not more than ten remained. It was a silly thing and I fought against it. I tried to stop the mental calculation. But it was no good.

We wound slowly down, trying not to look below us, trying not to think of what would happen if we should slide or skid. And within my mind a terrible fantasy built up. What would happen to us if somewhere the trail should happen to be broken? There is little change upon the Moon, but it's not impossible. What would we do if suddenly before us we found a gap in the trail that we could not cross? We'd be trapped without a single prayer. I sweated as I thought of trying to back up the trail to the rim again.

We were halfway down when Brill jogged my elbow.

"What?" I asked, exasperated at his bothering me.

"There," he said excitedly pointing.

I didn't look immediately. I flashed my stop light to warn Amelia's rig behind me. I cut the power and put light, even pressure on the brakes. The rig came to a halt. I glanced around. Amelia's rig had stopped, fifty feet behind, and I could see her face peering out at us.

"There," insisted Brill. "Over there, just beyond, the mountain."

I looked and saw it.

"What is it?" Brill demanded. "A cloud? A light?"

"It could have been either one. But there are no clouds on the Moon. Neither are there lights, unless they're man-made lights.

This thing was big—it had to be, to be seen at all— for it was at the far end of the crater, beyond the central mountain. It was a fiery thing that rolled against the distant peaks. It would look momentarily like fleecy clouds, then it would twinkle and flash, and then suddenly grow dark and then flash again, like a monstrous diamond that had caught a ray of light.

"They were right," said Brill, the breath whistling sharply in his teeth. "It is no fairy tale. There is really something there."

"This is the first time I have seen it."

"But you see it now."

"Yes," I said. "I see it."

And I was cold all over—cold with a greater fear than the fear of going down the rim.

"How far away?" asked Brill.

I shook my head. "Pretty far," I told him. "It looks to be against the farther wall. Fifty miles or more."

I looked around and waved to Amelia and pointed, and I saw her looking toward where I pointed. At first she didn't see it; then suddenly she did, for her hands went up to cup her face in a gesture close to terror.

We sat there watching.

It—whatever it might be—did not move. It stayed where it was. It throbbed and flashed and darkened.

"A signal," said Brill.

"What is it signaling to?"

"I wouldn't know," said Brill.

I released the brakes and let in the clutch and we moved forward once again.

It took hours, it seemed to me. When we reached

the crater floor, I was limp and sore from nervous tension. Big booby? Sure I am. So would anyone be.

I wheeled the rig around and craned my neck up at the crater wall and paid a silent tribute to the courage of that first man who had mapped out the trail.

"The cloud," said Brill, "went away a little while ago. I didn't mention it. I didn't want to bother you."

I got up and went to the refrigerator and took out the water bottle. I drank first, then handed it to Brill. It was rude, undoubtedly, but I needed water worse than he did.

He took a swallow or two, then handed it back.

I liked the way he did it. Not all Earthlubbers know that when you are Out Back you don't guzzle water. You always drink a little less than you really need.

I snapped down my helmet and crawled out the hatch. A minute after I dropped out, Amelia came crawling from her rig.

"What is it, Chris?" she asked.

She gestured with her arm.

"I don't know," I said.

Brill plopped from the hatch like something spit out by a slot machine. You have to get the knack of it; there are so many things on the Moon you have to get the knack of.

He got to his feet and went through the absurd motions of dusting himself off. Where he had lit there wasn't any dust.

But off to the right was a monstrous talus slide, the dust as fine as flour—pure rock dust flaked off and shriven off and pounded off the rocks above over the course of many millions of years.

Brill came up to us.

His big hearty voice came thundering on our radio: "Well, we made it. What do we do now?"

The high rocks above the talus slope were stained here and there with the dark splashes of the lichens, and a few hound dogs fluttered before the faces of the rock.

Susie perched on my shoulder, sparkling. Amelia's hound came over and the two of them played ring around a rosy.

I gestured toward the rocks. "There you are," I said to Brill.

"There'll be a lot of others," Amelia said impatiently.

"You have any idea what we should do next?" I asked.

"There's the old observatory site around here somewhere. If we could locate that . . ."

I nodded. "They'd have put in some stakes. And there might be tracks. we could follow those."

"You mean," said Brill, "the tracks of the men who turned up missing."

"That's right," I told him.

"But you two are looking for those ships."

"I have a hunch the tracks would lead straight to them."

"And then we disappear as well."

"Maybe," I said.

"And along the way," said Brill, "I study hounds and lichens."

"That's what you came here for."

"Oh, yes, of course," said Brill.

We got back into our rigs and cruised in a semi-circle, and a little distance out we found tracks going west, close against the wall—not a lot of tracks, just tracks here and there where there happened to be dust.

We followed the tracks.

We came at last to the observatory site. There were a lot of tracks. There were stakes driven in the ground with the red flags hanging limply. There were stacks of supplies. There were scattered instruments. The site lay in a bay carved into the wall, with great black cliffs rising straight up from the plain. It was an eerie place. It set your teeth on edge. There are a lot of places on the Moon that by their sheer stark loneliness set your teeth on edge.

And leading southward across the crater floor were many tracks, all headed purposefully toward the central mountain.

We swung our rigs around and took out along the tracks. We made good time, the two rigs running abreast across the flat floor of the crater. There were places where we had to swing around minor crater-lets. We hit one crevasse that forced us to take a wider detour.

It had been all damn foolishness, I told myself, to start out as late as this. We should have waited until morning so that we'd have fourteen Earth days of light to carry out our venture. But our hand had been forced by Amelia's situation. She was illegal as all hell, and even I could have found a place to hide her out in Coonskin, the situation would very likely have gotten stickier. For sooner or later Coonskin Central would have found that she'd slipped through their clutches and would be hunting her.

We went rolling across the flat, with the great walls and the jagged peaks of the crater wall every way you looked, with the sun beating down and blinding bright even through the filters of the visiplate, with the cluck and chuckle of the radiation counter beating out a warning undertone, with Susie jigging up and down atop the radio and shooting out small and discreet showers of sparks. The land and the time stretched out forever and there was no end to anything, but an eternity of blinding light and darkling shadow and the utter sense of lifelessness and the great sterility.

Brill broke the spell.

He grabbed me by the shoulder.

"Over there!" he shouted. "Over there!"

I saw it immediately and slammed on the brakes.

Amelia, slightly behind us, came skidding to our side.

It lay out there, lonely in the dust, a sprawling thing and limp, with the sun sparkling on the helmet and one arm outstretched.

I shut off the turbines and scrambled for the hatch, and even as I did I knew there was no need of haste. For the thing that lay out there had been there these many years.

CHAPTER SIX

HE HAD died face downward, and in the last mo-
ments of his life he had found the time and strength
to reach out his arm and, with a finger for a pencil,
write the message in the dust.

And if he had been lucky the message would have
stayed there, fresh and legible as the day he'd written,
for half eternity. But the dancing dust motes, stirred
by the breathing wrath of the distant sun, had almost
erased his work.

Almost.

Not quite.

For two words remained:

NO DIAMONDS

And a little way beneath the words, as if it were
part of another sentence, were three letters, not a
word:

TER

And that was all there was.

"Poor devil," Brill said, looking at him.

I went down on one knee and reached out my hands to touch him, and Amelia said, "Leave him there. Exactly as he is."

And I saw that she was right. There was nothing we could do. There was nothing he would have wanted us to do.

He was dead. There was no need to look upon his face, dried and desiccated, mummified by the aridness that in a little time would have sucked up every drop of moisture, even through the protection of the suit.

"He must have been one of the rescue party," I said. "One of those who went out to find the missing survey party."

For otherwise someone would have found and moved him, and it was evident that he had lain there undisturbed since that hour when he had stumbled and been unable to get up. Or, perhaps more truly, since that hour when he had given up and refused to face any longer the pitiless thing that fought him. He had written out his message and then had lain there, in the great silence and the vast uncaring, waiting for the end.

I got up and moved into the shadows of the rigs, out of the terrible heat. The others joined me and we stood there, looking at him.

"That's a strange message," Brill observed, "for

a dying man to write. No diamonds. When you are facing death you think of other things than diamonds."

"It may have been a warning," Amelia said. "A warning to others who might have heard a rumor. A warning that there were no diamonds. No use of going further, for there are no diamonds."

I shook my head, perplexed. "There has never been a rumor such as that," I said. "I have never heard it and I've heard every rumor, I am sure, that ever circulated in Coonskin. I've heard all sorts of rumors but never one like that. Never any rumors of diamonds to be found in Tycho."

"Even if there were," said Brill, "how could he be sure? He could not have explored all of Tycho. He wouldn't have the time."

"How do we know?" I asked. "There is no way of knowing how long he might have been there."

"And the rest of it," Amelia whispered. "Those three other letters . . ."

"After." said Brill. "Or water. Or matter, They could be almost anything. It's a common ending for a lot of words."

"Or the beginning," I said. "It could have been terrain."

"I don't think," said Brill, "he would have used a word like that. He would have used simple words. He'd have striven to be simple and direct. He knew that he was dying. He knew he had no time and probably very little strength. And he may have been half crazy."

I walked out of the shade, back to the suited corpse again, and bent down, studying the dust where the message had been written. But there was nothing to be seen, nothing to be learned. There was not the faintest trace of other lettering. The eraser had wiped clean.

And it might as well, I thought a little bitterly, have wiped it clean entirely for all the good it did us. It was infuriating when you thought about it. There had been a message here, an important message. Or at least a message a dying man had believed to have enough importance to be written out in hope that it might help another man in another day.

In that message, it seemed to me, rested a certain symbolism of man's ever-springing optimism, of his terrible certainty, of his arrogant sense of continuity— that even on the edge of death he should attempt to communicate, even in a place like this, even in the desolation and the nakedness of a basic and primal hostility that waited patiently to suck the life from him, confident and sure that in the days to come some other man would read what he had written, contemptuous even then of the thing that was slowly killing him, knowing that other men would conquer it.

I turned around and walked back toward the rig. Amelia and Brill were staring at the sky.

I walked up beside them.

"They're at it again," said Brill.

The cloud was there again, I saw, rolling and flashing in the sky. Like a light house, like a signal, like a lamp set in a window.

And it was creepy. It was worse even than the silence, or the whiteness and the blackness; worse than the great uncaring.

I wondered what Brill had meant by *they*. With what agency or force did he equate the cloud? Or was he only trying to make the horror more familiar by personalizing it?

It was on the tip of my tongue to ask him and then I didn't ask him. I don't know why I didn't. It was almost as if it would have been like reaching down into the soul of him with an unclean hand and fishing for a part of him no man was meant to see.

I stood for a moment with the others, watching the flashing and the rolling in the sky; then I turned away.

"We'll grab a bite to eat," I said, "and get a few hours sleep. Then we'll hit the road again."

And this was it, I thought. This was the final lap.

CHAPTER SEVEN

THE WALLS reared up a thousand feet or more to frame the gateway, and the tracks led through the gateway. There were many tracks now and in the dust and softer rubble they had fashioned ruts. Here all the many vehicles which had rolled toward oblivion had converged to go into the funnel of the gateway.

I pulled the rig up to a halt and waited for Amelia to pull up beside us.

You could almost smell a trap. But that, I told myself, was completely foolish, for there was nothing on the Moon to trap you. Nothing but the Moon itself, that fantastic chunk of *outré* real estate. Although there were the hound dogs and the lichens, but the lichens were only a peculiar sort of plant that was lousy with a peculiar kind of microbe and the hounds were—what? Chunks of living energy? Thoughtful will-o'-the-wisps? Sentient Roman candles? God knows what they were, or what purpose they might have. Or why they lived or how. Or why one of them should attach itself to a living being, like a faithful pet.

I looked at the walls again and they were dark, since they lay in shadow, and they went up and up like carven monoliths, and far above, on their summits, I could catch the glitter of the sunlight glancing off their tops.

I looked across at Amelia and she made a motion, waving her hand forward to let me know it was all right with her—that we should go ahead.

I put the rig in gear and crept slowly forward between the two rock walls. It was a sterile place, simply the walls coming down on either side, with the rubble in between.

The corridor went straight ahead and I wondered what geologic highjinks must have been performed to bring it into being, to split the cliffs and carve this passageway. On Earth it could have been cut by water, but at no time in its history had the Moon ever had the water that would have been necessary to chew out such a canyon. It might have been a lunarquake or, once again, it might have been some fantastic happenstance that came about when the monstrous meteor which had punched out Tycho had impacted on the surface.

The pathway curved gently to the right, then

abruptly to the left, and, as I made the left-hand turn, the fierce light of the sun struck full into our faces. After the dark, even with the filters slid in place, the light was a blinding shock and it was a little time before I could make out where we were.

Then I saw that we were in what might have been another crater, although the surrounding wall seemed to be too straight for it to be a crater. There was no slope at all, just the walls, rising stark and perpendicular from a floor almost as smooth as a living room. And rising from the smoothness of the floor, the strange typical Moon formation—the crazy, jagged peaklets that looked like a melted candle, the tiny craterlets, the obscene-looking mounds, and the crisscross of tiny crevasses. The walls ran in a semicircle, backed against the natural crater wall itself, towering far above the straighter walls, but sloped instead of straight. And I knew, looking at it, that this was the southern slope of Tycho, that we had come all the way across the crater.

But that wasn't all.

There, in the center of the area, sat two spaceships—red bodies with gray domes, spraddling on four landing gears. And scattered all about them were moon rigs, gleaming in the glare of the sun.

And other things—other huddled bundles lying helter-skelter.

But the spaceships and the rigs and the huddled bundles did not immediately register upon my brain as actual things. Rather, the thought that came crashing down was that Amelia had been right. There had never been a time, I suppose, up to this very moment, when I actually had been convinced we would find the spaceships of the lost Third Lunar Expedition. I had, actually, scarcely thought of it; I had not debated it; I had neither accepted nor rejected it. It had been a pleasant El Dorado; it had been a magnificent will-o'-the-wisp to chase across the outlawed floor of Tycho.

And I wondered as I sat there, staring at the ships, if that, after all, had been the reason I had come; if this whole crazy expedition, on my part, had been no more than a gesture of rebellion against the Moon itself. One could come to resent the Moon; one could come to hate the Moon without really knowing it.

I pulled ahead, as I did I realized for the first time—although the knowledge must have struck me the instant I saw them—that huddled shapes were spacesuits. Here, after many years, were all the men who had been lost in Tycho.

These men and two others—the man who had scrawled the message out on the crater floor, and the man who had been found by Amelia's brother on the outer slope.

There was danger here. There was evidence of death and danger there before our eyes. And there was the sense of danger and the breath of danger in the very place itself.

With an involuntary cry of warning, I twisted on the wheel to swing the machine around, to head back through the passageway between the walls, to get out of there as fast as the rig would take me.

And even as I did there was a flash of fire—so rapid that one could little more than sense it, so intense that it was momentarily blinding—and the rig went dead.

Brill had fallen backward off his seat and now he sat grotesquely on the floor, with one arm across his face to shut out the flare that was gone entirely now. Smoke streamed out of the instrument board and there was the acrid smell of burned installation and of melted metal.

Susie was fluttering excitedly in the center of the cabin.

"Quick!" I yelled. "Outside!"

I hauled Brill off the floor and slapped his helmet down, pushed him toward the hatch. He scrambled blindly into it and I followed close behind.

Amelia's rig stood twenty feet away and I raced toward it, yelling for Brill to follow me.

But it was no use.

Amelia was crawling from the hatch and through the visiplate I could see the wisps of smoke rising from the panel—the brand new panel that we'd installed not too many hours before.

We stood in stricken silence, the three of us together.

We were stranded here, on the farthest side of Tycho's crater, with no conceivable way of getting out.

Unless we tried walking it.

And we'd seen—all of us had seen—out on the crater's floor, what had happened to a man who tried walking out.

"Look," said Brill, pointing upward.

We looked.

The cloud was in the sky again—the cloud that we had seen off and on all across the crater.

It was no cloud at all.

It was millions upon millions of the hound dogs, dancing all together.

CHAPTER EIGHT

THEY HAD landed, I thought, and it had been fine. Earth had been hanging there, just above the horizon, as it was hanging now. And they had done a great thing. They were second on the Moon. For the First Lunar Expedition had been the only one so far to land and they'd stayed only for a week. And the Second Expedition had gone to pot in a spectacular, blazing glory when it was only halfway there.

But the men of the Third had come to set up base, they had come to stay. In a month or so another expedition would come plunging down out of the sky, carrying more supplies and further personnel.

The Third had come to stay, and they had stayed in all grim reality. For they still were here.

In that moment of their pride, a terrible thing had happened. The electrical circuits of their ships had flared and smoked and there had been miles of molten, twisted wires in the innards of those wonderful machines which had brought them here and which would never run again short of complete rewiring. And they didn't have the know-how and they didn't have the wire and they didn't have the time.

Their ships were grounded and their radios were dead, and they might have tried to reach Earth with small auxiliary sets (for we had found the sets), but it was no good. So they were isolated men, shipwrecked on a cosmic desert island—and by simply looking up they could see their planet and their home in the sky above them. And they would have known that they could never reach it.

With two expeditions gone, with only one success, Earth had been cautious about sending out another. It had been almost ten years before another expedition had gone out, equipped with what were then considered very foolproof ships. And they had not been foolproof, but they had been better. It was from this Fourth Expedition that the colonization of the Moon had finally dated.

And what had it been that had washed out the circuits, not only of the ships, but of the moon rigs of those others who had been lured here—and last of all, ourselves?

It made no sense at all, and the Moon had, in all the times before, made sense. Cruel it might be, barren, lonesome, hard—but it had made an uncaring sort of sense. It had no dirty tricks hidden up its sleeve, it had no sly and clever ambush; it was just a hard old girl to get along with, but entirely honest.

I got up from where I had been sitting in the shade of one of the rigs. It was late afternoon and the blaze of the sun was hot. A man had to get into the shade every now and then.

Soon, I knew, we had to work out a plan of action. We couldn't wait much longer. We had checked all the possibilities and not a one paid out. All the wiring in the ships was gone, and in the rigs as well. There was no hope of getting wire enough to patch up our own rigs. And even if we had, there was the very present question of how much good it might accomplish. For whatever had burned out the circuits in the first place, could burn them out again.

And here we stood, surrounded by all sorts of vehicles and not a single one among them that would turn a wheel.

We had found other things, of course.

The wall of the crater was draped and hung with lichens. There were more lichens here than I ever had imagined anyone would ever find. There were enough of them to run Doc's sanitarium for a thousand years or so, even if he threw a bunch of wings on it and took in more patients.

There were papers in the ship—the entire history of the expedition—as well as instruments and all sorts of other high-priced junk.

There was a fortune here, in salvage and in lichens

if one could get it out. But at the moment we'd be lucky to get out with our skin intact.

And there were dead men all around—the very ancient dead—most decently entombed in the coffins of their suits. But, somehow or other, quite impersonal. For there was no violence, nor any sign of it, and the agony was hidden by the bulky suits and the filter plates. They had died, it seemed on the face of it, with a quite Roman dignity that fitted in most admirably with the austere circumstances.

And that, I knew, was hogwash, but I inquired no further. It was less disturbing not to.

And there were the hound dogs, swarming all around, bright, shining little idiots that were quite unhelpful.

Brill came around one of the spaceships and walked over to me. He stopped in front of me and we stood facing one another.

"We'll have to make a move before too long," he said. "We can't just stay here and . . ."

He made a sweeping motion with his hand.

I knew what he meant. He didn't have to tell me. The man was terribly on edge. He was all upset. But so were Amelia and I.

"In just a while," I told him. "It looks as if we walk. We'll wait until the sun gets lower. You saw what happened to that guy out in the crater. He tried it in the daytime."

"But the dark . . ."

84

"Not as dark as you think. There'll be earthlight and it's a good deal brighter than the best moonlight on Earth. And it will be cool. It will even be cold. But we have heaters in our suits. You can fight the cold better than the heat."

"Jackson, tell me. What are our chances?"

"It's seventy miles," I said. "And the climb out of the crater. That will be a rough one."

He shook his head, discouraged.

"We'll get some sleep," I told him. "We'll start out fresh. We'll have to carry as much oxygen as we can to start with. But we'll discard the tanks as we go along. That will lighten up the load."

"Water?"

"You can carry only so much of it in a suit. And you can't replenish it. But we'll be traveling cold. We won't need as much as if we tried it in the heat."

He looked at me long and hard, with a glitter in his eyes. "You don't think that we will make it."

"It's never been done," I said. "Not seventy miles of walking in a spacesuit."

"Maybe someone will pick us up. They know by now we're missing. They'll be out looking. They'll know where we went. They'll spot the trailer on the rim."

"That's right."

"But you aren't counting on it."

I shook my head.

"How much longer?"

"Ten or twelve hours. We want to let it begin to cool off. There'll be time to get some sleep. There'll be time for you to take a good look at the lichens."

"I've looked at them," he said. "And the hound dogs. Jackson, was there ever a time when you were utterly baffled? When nothing made any sense at all?"

"Lots of times. This setup, for example."

"This," said Brill, "is where it all started—the hound dogs and the lichens. I am sure of it. This is the home ground for them. But why? How is this one place different than any other place upon the Moon?"

"I don't think it is," I said. "Take a look at these walls."

"What about the walls?"

"They aren't natural. They're straight. They're symmetrical. They seem to have a function. The Moon is haphazard, but these walls are not."

"You mean someone built these walls?"

"Maybe."

He nodded idly and moved closer to me. His voice dropped almost to a conspiratorial level, as if he were afraid someone might listen in.

"The lichens could be what's left of the kitchen garden. All that was left. All that survived."

"You've been thinking the same thing."

"Someone or something from outside," he said. "Maybe a million years ago."

"And the hounds?"

"Lord, how should I know? Pets, maybe. A few pets were left behind and they multiplied."

"Or watchers."

He looked at me with baffled worry in his eyes. "It sounds so logical," he said. "But of course it's speculation."

"Naturally," I said.

"There's one thing that bothers me," he said, and you could see that he was worried in a deeply academic way.

"There's a lot that worries me," I told him.

"It's the electrical failure," he said. "The failure is not random."

"Huh?"

"Well, the circuits in the rigs went out, but not those in our suits. The circuits in the ships out there went blooey, but not the circuits in some auxiliary radios. The ones they used to try to signal Earth. The failure is selective. It's not something that blankets all circuits."

"You mean intelligence."

"That is what I mean," said Brill.

I felt a chill wind blowing and there's no wind on the Moon.

For if there was intelligence it was an intelligence that wanted to keep us here, wanted us to stay and die, just like all these others had done.

"It doesn't stand to reason," said Brill, "that this life is native to the Moon. If life had risen on the

Moon it would have risen in more than one place. It does not make sense that there is only one place on its entire surface where life is possible."

"What about those pre-life molecules?"

"Yes, of course, they found them. But in every case that was all they found. The molecules fell into a dead end. They never did develop. The Moon was sterile even in its infancy. It offered no encouragement to life. It—"

The shout came loud and clear. It was Amelia calling.

"Chris, come quick! Chris! Chris!"

She was excited. Not frightened, but excited.

I swung around and there she was just out from the farther wall.

I ran and Brill pounded at my heels and I saw it even before I reached Amelia.

It stood in a little rock niche carved out from the wall and it shone with a million secret fires that lanced out purest light.

It was boulder size—a very massive boulder—and there was no mistaking what it was.

"A diamond!" Amelia sobbed. "The man out there was wrong.

And she was entirely right. The man out there was wrong.

For there stood the biggest diamond that ever had been found. Tons and tons of diamond!

But there was something else that was very wrong.

For the diamond was cut and faceted and polished and the living light of it flowed from every carven face.

And another thing.

We had covered the area a dozen times. We had walked around the walls. We had inspected the ships and had a look at all the rigs, hoping in a futile sort of way that we might find from them a clue that might be of help to us.

And we had not seen the diamond until this very moment, and it was not the sort of thing that could very well be missed.

There was something rotten here—and something very sneaky. As if the diamond might be a very special bait for some diabolic trap.

Brill stepped forward and I grabbed him by the arm.

"Stay back, you fool!" I told him.

For suddenly I knew what the dead man out on the crater floor had written. There had been enough space between the words for another letter.

Not diamonds is what he'd really written, rather than *no diamonds*. The little dancing dust motes had wiped out the letter *t*.

And even as we stood and watched, the diamond came apart.

Interlocking fist-size crystals peeled away and floated free in space. Slowly, methodically, almost mathematically, crystals peeled away until there was no diamond, but just a cloud of crystals floating there before our eyes, bumping gently together, and each one of them a blaze of light that almost put out your eyes.

We backed away from them and they floated slowly along the wall until they came to the passageway that led outside to the crater floor. And there they hung, like a door, like a curtain, quivering and waiting. You could feel them watching.

And that was why, I knew, no one had escaped from here—no one but the man we'd found and the other found by Amelia's brother.

"Well," I said, "they've really got us now."

I should not have said it. I don't know why I said it. But it seemed so logical and true I could not help the saying. The words suddenly were there, formed inside my brain, and they popped out of my mouth.

And at the sound of them, Brill screamed and ran—running desperately, head down, boots kicking up great clots of rubble, shoulders hunched, as if he were a football player who meant to crack the line. Straight for the passageway he went, heading out for freedom, breaking from the trap in a sheer rush of insane desperation.

Two crystals spun out from the curtain and were twin streaks of flashing lights as they bulleted for Brill. They hit and ricocheted, spiraling upward, flashing as they spun, and Brill was stumbling. He hit the ground and crawled ahead a ways, then fell into a heap and slumped into a stillness.

The curtain shimmered and a cloud of hounds came down, like a cloud of vultures, and settled on the man lying on the ground, settling so thickly that he was lost from sight and all that remained to see was a million sparks that danced and scintillated.

I turned away and bumped into Amelia.

Her eyes were large and frightened and her face was deathly pale.

"God save us now," she said.

CHAPTER NINE

So THERE WERE three of them, whatever they might be: the diamond and the lichens and the hounds.

Amelia said, "I got you into this."

I said, "I wasn't hard to get. I almost jumped at it."

And that was true. I had. It was a chance to really lay my hands on something; it was the chance to clean up big. And those chances didn't come too often; you grabbed them when they came.

And more than that. It was an answer to the men sitting in the Millville barber shop, snapping their suspenders. And it was Brill asking how much it would take for me to take him into Tycho when I'd been scheming all the while to run from him to Tycho. And it had been insurance against walking down the streets of Millville, glad to take any job that anyone might offer.

Nor was that all of it, either, I told myself, being really honest. It had been, as well, an excuse to come stumbling into Tycho. To come and see the place that was talked about in whispers. For Tycho was a haunted house, and for certain kinds of people haunted houses have a fatal fascination. I guess I was that kind of person.

The cabin of the rig was hot, but the long shadow from the wall would reach it in a while and then it would cool off; and it was a comfort, it was almost a necessity, to get the helmet off. A man can go raving crazy if he's caged in it too long.

"We really aren't going to get out of it," Amelia said. "You don't really think we are."

"I haven't given up," I said. "Once you give up, you're dead. There may be a way we haven't thought of yet."

"I threw away the old panel," Amelia said, "I should have hung onto it. But there is so little room."

"It would have done no good," I told her. "It's not just the panel. It's all the wiring. Just the panel by itself would have done no good. And even if we had it now and could get it in and had all the wiring, there's not a thing to stop them from blowing it again."

To stop them? To stop who or what?

The diamond, more than likely. And the diamond still was out there. I could see it out there. It had gone back together and was a boulder once again. It sat there proud and beautiful and just slightly vulgar for its very bigness. It was sitting there and watching. It was the garrison. It was the garrison left behind to guard this bleak and minor outpost of some empire that a human being, in his provinciality, could not even guess at. It was the ancient legion that sat atop the wall, forgotten in the drift of cosmic affairs, but remaining loyal and steadfast.

Although maybe not forgotten, for there could be no knowing how many other garrisons stood guard in other places as inhospitable as this.

And I knew, even as I thought it, that I was guilty of too-human thinking—for while the Moon was in all conscience inhospitable to humans, it might seem quite homelike to another being. To a crystal being like the diamond. To an energy being, like the hounds. Even to a queer symbiotic being, composed of plant and bacteria, like the lichens.

Earth might be a planet which would seem most inhospitable to such as these. Air and water might be absolute poison to them.

"I am sorry, Chris," Amelia said.

"Sorry?"

"Sorry that we aren't going back. We could have had a drink or two together, we could have gone to dinner, perhaps we even could have . . ."

"Yes," I said, "I think we could have."

We looked at one another solemnly.

"Kiss me, Chris," she said.

I did. It was rather awkward business in a space-suit, but very satisfactory.

"You've been an all right guy," she said.

"Thanks," I told her. "Thank you very much."

Brill's suited body still lay just inside the gateway. There had been no reason why we should have moved it. It was in good company. After the hounds had taken leave, I'd had a look at him. The crystals had hit his helmet and two neat holes had been punched into the heavy glass. Little radiating fracture lines ran out from each of them. And those holes had been enough. The oxygen had poured out and Brill had quickly died. His face was not a pretty thing to look at.

And why had Brill run? I wondered. What had panicked him? He was not a man to panic, and yet perhaps he was. More than likely that quite academic manner was no better than a post to hide the fear that was building up in him. And when he saw the last route of escape being finally plugged, he had made his break. It had been a foolish thing to do. No Moonman would have done it. But Brill was not a Moonman; he was fresh from Earth. And just the Moon itself is enough to panic someone who is not acclimated to it.

There was something I had thought just a minute before, something that had gone rattling through my skull that I should have caught a hold on. Something about the Moon being home to a certain breed and the Earth a home to yet another breed. . . .

I sat and thought about it, not nearly as excited as I should have been, and it was a gamble. It was a crazy sort of gamble. It could turn out, if it failed, to be a very deadly gamble. But we were dead in any event if the diamond held the gateway and a failing gamble would only make it quicker. And we had no time to lose. If we were going to get out of here, we must be leaving soon.

I went to the cupboard and hunted through a drawer until I found an old can-opener and I put it in my pocket.

"Come on, Amelia," I said. "We're getting out of here."

She gave me a funny look, but she didn't argue. She didn't want to know how we were getting out of anything like that.

She started for the hatch and I followed her.

Amelia's rig still had tanks of oxygen and cans of water lashed down on the outer deck. We got down four tanks and rigged them with ropes so we could grab them up and sling them from our shoulders.

We carried them as close to the gateway as we dared, not wanting to rouse the watching diamond. But we needn't have worried any. All it did was squat there and watch us with its thousand glittering eyes.

We went back and broke out fresh tanks and replaced those on our suits so we could start out—if we started out—with a full supply.

Then we got down the water tins and I got out the can opener and went after them. A spacesuit is an awkward thing at best. It was never meant to operate an opener on a tin.

But finally I wrangled the top off two of them. I spilled a little water, but not very much. It slopped out of the cans and spilled onto the ground. It soaked into the ground and left a wet spot there and it broke my heart, almost, for it was an awful sight. Water is something you don't spill out in the wilderness.

I straightened up from the second can and put the opener back into my pocket.

"Chris," Amelia said, "what is it all about?"

"Two barrels," I said. "A double-barreled shotgun. We have just two chances."

"Oxygen and water."

"That is exactly it. One or the other of them might scare it off a bit so we can make a dash."

We picked up a tank of oxygen and a tin of water. Amelia took the other tin.

We walked up close this time and the diamond sat there, staring at us—or I suppose that it was staring at us—maybe even wondering what we might be up to. But it wasn't worried. It had no need to worry. This was not the first time it had dealt with humans and it was not afraid of them. They were soft and weak and very, very stupid and there was nothing they could do to hurt the diamond any.

I put my can of water down on the ground and

hitched the oxygen tank around. I got my feet set hard against the ground and I grasped the valve and pointed the connection nozzle directly at the diamond. Then I twisted the valve as hard as I could twist it, and the tank bucked in my arm and slammed against my shoulder as the oxygen poured out.

Nothing happened for a moment. The gush of gas stirred some dust to life and raised a tiny cloud, but the diamond did not move. Then slowly, almost insolently, it began to come apart. For it had had enough of it. This tiny, squalid human could not blow into its face. It would teach it not to do so.

"Amelia" I shouted.

Amelia was ready and she let the diamond have five gallons of good wet water right smack in its face.

A second dragged out to half eternity and then the diamond steamed. It smoked and ran and blurred. It began to melt. White salts ran down its sides. It began to slump into a dreadful shapelessness.

I dropped the oxygen tank and it writhed away, the last of the gas inside it propelling it along the ground on an erratic course. I grabbed up my can of water, but I didn't throw it. I halted it even as I began to throw it. For there wasn't any need.

The diamond was a heap of powdery substance that steamed a little, settling in upon itself.

Our second barrel had paid off where the first had failed. Oxygen was as nothing to this alien being, but water had been deadly.

"Exorcised," I said, talking to myself.

Exorcised by water, and not even holy water.

Sent back into nothingness by an alien and a hostile and a very deadly substance that another race could not live without.

And that, I told myself, was the gulf that lay between us and these other things—that our very common needs should be unknown to either of the other.

I glanced back over my shoulder and the jaggedness of the crater's rim was already cutting into the shimmer of the sun.

"Amelia," I said, "it is time for us to go."

We picked up the tanks and heaved them on our shoulders and went plodding down the passageway and out into the crater.

Far ahead we saw the whiteness of the farther rim and it was a long way off.

Dark was coming down and soon it would be cooler and then it would be cold. But the good old Earth would light us on our way.

And we had found our treasure. There were millions back there for us—if we could make it out to Coonskin.

We plodded on, side by side, making fairly good time. A spacesuit is a miserable thing to walk in, but once you hit your stride you can do a fair job of getting over ground. Especially on a body like the Moon, where the lesser gravity gives you something of an edge.

"Chris," Amelia said, "that's what the other word meant."

"What other word?"

"The word the man wrote in the dust. There was just part of it."

"*Ter,*" I said.

"Don't you see. He had written *water.*"

"Maybe so," I said.

Although she was mistaken, I was sure. It could have been anything at all. It needn't have been *water*.

I wished she hadn't mentioned it. I didn't like to think about it. It was too personal.

I broke my stride and swung around to have a final look at the beetling walls behind which had been hidden the mystery of Tycho.

And as I looked at them, I saw something else.

Streaming out above them, in a painted streamer that hung against the sky, following on our trail, came a cloud of hound dogs.

And I noticed something else. Susie was no longer with us nor was Amelia's hound. They had deserted us and now the entire pack of them was baying at our heels.

CHAPTER TEN

I DUG a hole in the talus slope and dragged Amelia into it. Using my hands, I covered her with dust, all except her head. There still was heat below the top layer of the dust, left over from the pounding sunlight of the lunar day—and the dust as well would act as insulation.

Now the Moon was cold. The sun had been gone for hours and the heat, except for the little trapped within the piles of dust accumulated at the bottoms of steep slopes, had fled into outer space. The heaters in our suits were unable to hold off the cold entirely. It was all right as long as one was walking, for then the increased body heat, held in by the suit, became a warming factor. But it would have been suicide to stop and rest without the added insulation and the trapped heat of the dust.

I patted down the dust and rose unsteadily to my

feet and every muscle screamed. It had been that way for hours, for we had not dared to stop until we reached this place where we would find the massive piles of dust.

Inch by inch I straightened until I stood erect. Then I wheeled awkwardly around and glanced back the way we'd come, and there lay all the plains of Tycho—the whole fifty miles of them. And we had come that way without a second's sleep. We'd made two stops to rest before the nighttime cold clamped down, but those two stops had been the only breaks we'd had. It seemed impossible when I thought back on it, and I knew the only reason we had been able to make it had been because the going had been good. The crater floor was smooth; there were craterlets that must be walked around, and the lumps and mounds and fantastic candles that one had to dodge, but the floor itself was smooth. It was not the hell-broth tangle that one found in much of the wilderness Out Back.

The hounds still hung above us in a glittering cloud. They had paced us all the way. It was if some guardian entity was hanging there above us.

I bent above Amelia's helmet and I could see that she was sleeping. And that was fine, because she needed sleep. Out on her feet for the last five miles or more, she had made it this far only by the last thin edge of courage. And a lot of heckling by me. I wouldn't blame her, I told myself, if she never spoke to me again—the way I'd talked to her.

I got down on my knees and began to dig a hole I could crawl into myself. There I could rest and the heat would keep me warm, but I must not go to sleep. I had to stay awake, for there was a chance that if we stayed too long, we would stay forever. Eventually the heat would seep out from the dust and the cold would drive down in and, when that happened, it would be death to stay there.

I dug the hole and crawled into it, then pawed the dust back on top of me. I lay there, staring at the cliffs above us.

Twelve thousand feet, I thought. And when we made that twelve thousand feet, our worries would be over. For the trailer would be there and we could get into it and finally be safe.

There might be a rescue party too, but that didn't really matter, for the trailer was enough.

I wondered vaguely why the rescue party (for surely there had been one out for hours) had not come down into the crater. And I realized there were two perfectly good reasons for their not doing so.

They would have seen the tracks going down into the crater, but they would not have been able to know that they were new tracks. There is no way on the Moon to tell new tracks from old—they both are just as fresh. But the time the rescue party arrived, a few meteorites would have fallen and punched their tiny craters in the tracks we'd made, a few patches of dust would have done their little dance and blotted out a tiny patch of track. And after that had happened there would have been no way to distinguish our tracks from the tracks of the rescue party which had gone out twenty years before and never come back.

And, likewise, the rescue party would have said among themselves: "Chris Jackson is an old hand. He'd never be damn fool enough to go blundering into Tycho."

So they'd not come into the crater, but had scattered to hunt the outer slopes.

I lay there and I caught myself a dozen times on the verge of sleep and found my way back to wakefulness.

The hounds were circling above me like a wheel of light, like a flight of buzzards, and it seemed to me that they were lower now than they had been before, as if they might be cautiously spiraling downward to have a closer look.

I watched them and the wheel of sparkling light had a terrible fascination, so I jerked my eyes away. And when I looked again the cloud of them was closer, much closer—almost on top of me.

One of them came down and roosted on the faceplate of my helmet, right before my eyes, and I knew that it was Susie. Don't ask me how or why I knew—I just knew that it was Susie. And she stayed there, dancing as if she might be happy that she'd found me once again. Then the others closed down on me until I could no longer pick out Susie, but only a universe of sparkling things that seemed to fill my very brain and being.

One sane thought intruded on my mind: This was the way they had closed in on Brill at the moment of his dying.

And I wasn't dead!

I wasn't even close to death!

I was going to crawl out of this bed of dust in just a little while and wake Amelia, and then the two of us together would climb twelve thousand feet to safety.

Twelve thousand feet. It sounded short, after fifty miles, but I didn't kid myself. That twelve thousand feet could be almost as tough as the fifty miles.

And we'd never make it. I might just as well go to sleep right now, for we would never make it.

But Susie was out there somewhere, tapping on the glass front of my helmet—or I thought she was tapping. And she was trying to talk to me, as she'd tried so many times before.

And something talked to me—maybe not Suisie, but something was out there. It talked in a thousand tongues and a million dialects, as if a crowd was talking to one person, speaking all at once. And speaking different things.

I knew it was for real. I wasn't dreaming, nor was I imagining, and I wasn't crazy. An old Moon-hand like me never does go crazy. If I'd been going to go crazy, I'd have done it long before.

"Hiya, pal," said the thing that was talking to me.

Then another one came up and took me by the hand and we walked along together beside a funny river, for the river was bright-blue liquid oxygen. Our feet went crunch as we walked along, and when I looked down and saw that we were walking on something that looked like a carpet of those kinds of balls you hang on Christmas trees.

Then another came up and grabbed me and took me someplace else, and this place seemed more like home than a bright-blue river, but the houses were all funny and the trees were out of shape and there were bugs the size of horses.

Someone talked to me in mathematics and, queer enough, I understood him. Another talked in the sound of tinkling crystals, and I understood him too; and I heard a lot of other voices that were sitting there and yarning and there wasn't a cracker barrel nor a pot-bellied stove, but there should have been. For they were telling stories and, while the details fuzzed on me, I could gain the drift of them, and they were all stories of long ago and far away—unimaginably far away.

But in the middle of it a voice said to me, "Chris, snap out of it. You have to get to Coonskin. You have to tell them what this is all about."

And it was not the words, but the voice itself, that snapped me out of it. For I recognized the voice. It was Brill who was talking to me, dead back there, fifty miles away.

I don't know how I got out of the dust so fast, but all at once I was on my feet and flapping my arms at a bunch of swirling hounds, like a man will swat at bees. They were whirling around, as if they were astonished that I didn't want them there. It took a while, but I finally drove them off. They went out of there like a flock of fireflies and formed in a cloud above me and everything was normal.

I hauled Amelia from the dust and stood her on her feet and shook her.

"Get awake," I told her. "Take a drink of water. We're getting out of here."

"Just a little while," she said. "Just a little while."

"Nothing doing, doll," I told her.

I got her headed for the trail and I kept her going and we started up that last twelve thousand feet.

I was scared. I was scared down to my heels. For I have no time for ghosts, and that is what the hound dogs were. Just a gang of ghosts.

I didn't have a body. I just had a pair of legs that ached, and every time one of them moved it had to lift a boot that had grown to weigh about a thousand pounds. But the legs did not belong to me. They were a part of me no longer. The "me" of me stood off a ways and it didn't care what happened to the legs and that way it kept them going.

We clawed our way up the trail. We walked when

we could, and the places that we couldn't walk we went on hands and knees.

But we never stopped. We did some slipping back at times, but we kept on going up.

For I had the crazy idea that, if we could reach the rim, the hounds would go away and bother us no longer.

Amelia sobbed part of the time, but I made her keep on going. She wanted to stop to rest, but I wouldn't let her do it. When she fell down, I picked her up and set her on her feet and shoved her from behind.

I know she hated me. She told me that she did.

It was damn undignified, but we went on up the trail.

I lost all track of time. I lost all sense of distance. The trail was something that went up and up forever.

So I was surprised—not happy or relieved or triumphant, but utterly surprised—when the trail pinched out before us and the land, instead of going up, went down.

A faint memory came to me that this had been our goal, that this finally was the place we had been headed for, that we won our way to safety.

Amelia had crumpled to the ground and I stood swaying there, with her huddled at my feet, and I hoped I had the strength to drag her to the trailer.

And there was something wrong, something deathly wrong. My brain was so fogged with weariness that it did not penetrate at once. But finally it did.

There wasn't any trailer?

I stood, staring at the place where we had parked it, and I knew I could not mistake the place. Someone had hitched it up and hauled it back to Coonskin.

This, I knew, was the end of it. It had been a lot of foolishness and utterly wasted effort for us to climb the trail. We might just as well have stayed down there, warm in our beds of dust, and gone peacefully to sleep.

For even if we could manage all the miles to Coonskin, our oxygen would not last.

I knew that we were beat.

I knew this time for sure.

I sat down stiffly on the ground beside Amelia.

I reached out a hand and patted her on the shoulder.

"I am sorry, lass," I said. "The trailer isn't here. It isn't working out."

She raised herself and crept over to me. I reached out an arm and dragged her close. She put her arm around me. It's not as romantic as it sounds. A spacesuit simply isn't something to do any necking in.

"I don't care," she said.

And I didn't either. Life, it seemed to me, was something not worth one's while to keep. Not if it meant another step, if it cost another minute without sleep; not if it exacted another fraction of one's energy.

I looked up at the sky and the hounds were there, waiting to come down.

"All right, you bastards," I told them. "We're ready now. Come and get us."

For it might not be so bad. There'd be a lot of company and a lot to talk about; there'd be a lot of yarns to spin. And, more than likely, a lot of people who'd be downright interesting. You might even get to like it—this business of the essence of you, the life of you, the soul of you, call it what you might, becoming encapsulated and unshrined, perhaps forever, in some sort of being that was pure energy.

It was not the Christian pattern; it wasn't even heathen; it was not the pattern of any Earthly thinking, but there it hung above us, an undoubted alien fact.

And among the host up there would be some Earthmen good and true—Brill, and the members of the Third Lunar Expedition, and the surveying crew, and those members of the rescue party who went out to hunt the surveying crew.

And who were the others? From what far stars? And to what purpose here?

The merry men of the universe? The hordes of outer space? The gentlemen adventurers of the galaxy?

And not above recruiting. Not above grabbing off another being when the chance presented. For it was entirely clear that they had trapped the lunar expedition, that they had lured the surveying crew, that they had led the rescue party on. And they had, as well, kept their hideout well concealed from any passing ship, for a thin cloud of them, hovering above the hideout, would have blanked out the seeing without a doubt.

They were the ones, I thought. They were the intelligences which were behind it all. The diamond had been no more than a convenient adjunct, snatched perhaps for its usefulness from some unguessed planet on an unseen star. And the lichens—could the lichens be the trap that they had set for men, for the men who hunted them, knowing that sooner or later someone would come seeking the lichens' source and become another victim?

"Robin Hood," I said.

"What were you saying, Chris?"

"Just thinking. An old story I read when I was young."

The cloud was settling down and there was no need, I told myself, for further speculation. In just a while all the questions could be asked and all the answers told.

I tightened my arm around Amelia and she murmured something at me that I didn't catch. And all the time the hounds were setting like a golden shower.

They had almost reached us when a brilliant light sprang out and caught us in its center, a blazing, blinding light that came from down the slope.

I scrambled to my feet and behind the light I saw the dark shape of a rig, crunching up the slope.

I dragged Amelia up.

"Someone came for us!" I shouted.

But the shout wasn't a great deal better than a raspy, worn-out whisper.

The rig swung broadside to us and we staggered toward the hatch. I boost Amelia up and waited while she clawed her way inside.

I glanced upward as I waited and saw that the hounds were climbing slowly upward.

I waved a hand at them.

"Another time," I told them.

Then I clambered through the hatch.

I crawled out on the floor and got to my knees. I snapped my helmet back and drew in a breath of fresh air that felt so good it almost strangled me.

And there was Doc Withers, twice as big as life, leaning on the control panel and happy as a fool.

"You!" I blurted.

He grinned like a drunken pixie.

"Did you find them?" he demanded. "Did you find the lichens?"

"Tons of them," I said. "More than you can ever use."

"The others said you'd never go near Tycho. They said you were too smart for that. But I knew you had. I knew, when I talked with you the other day, that you'd go hunting them."

"Look, Doc," I grasped. "We weren't . . ."

"I stayed and waited here for you," said Doc, "while the others went out on the slope. But finally it got so late I thought you weren't coming. So I headed on back home. Then my conscience got to bothering me. What if I left just half an hour too soon? I asked myself. What if Chris showed up ten minutes after I had left? So I turned around and came back to see if you were here."

"Thank you, Doc," I said.

"And," said Doc, with an archness that ill-befitted him, "who might this lady be?"

I looked at Amelia. She had her helmet off and I saw, for the first time, I think, how beautiful she was.

"Perhaps," I told him, "the richest person on the Moon this minute. The bravest. And the sweetest."

Amelia smiled at me.

AWARD-WINNING

Science Fiction!

The following titles are winners of the prestigious Nebula or Hugo Award for excellence in Science Fiction. A must for lovers of good science fiction everywhere!